Romantic Getaways
Escape to Paradise!

This Valentine's Day, escape to four of the world's
most romantic destinations with these sparkling
books from Harlequin Romance!

From the awe-inspiring desert to vibrant Barcelona,
from the stunning coral reefs of Australia to heart-
stoppingly romantic Venice, get swept away by
these wonderful romances!

The Sheikh's Convenient Princess
by Liz Fielding

The Unforgettable Spanish Tycoon
by Christy McKellen

The Billionaire of Coral Bay
by Nikki Logan

Her First-Date Honeymoon
by Katrina Cudmore

Dear Reader,

I've wanted to write an amnesia story for a while now and was ruminating on how to start it when a rather intriguing question popped into my head.

What might happen to someone who's harbored feelings of anger and hurt toward someone for years—that have tainted every relationship they've ever had—if they suddenly lost their memory and found themselves in their enemy's care?

And I was away.

At the heart of it, this story is about how determinedly clinging on to past hurts can stop you from moving forward with your life. In our hero, Caleb's, case it takes a potentially disastrous event to force him to reevaluate his life and help him see that holding on to anger and resentment is only going to cause him more pain and heartache and ultimately keep him apart from the love of his life. And for our heroine, Elena, it's the perfect way to finally atone for the wrongs she did Caleb by moving past her risk-averse tendencies to find the courage she needs in order to forgive herself—if she can only keep her heart intact in the process!

It's quite a journey for the two of them, full of uncertainty and trepidation as they push past deeply rooted behaviors, but also one filled with hope and excitement for the future. I hope you enjoy tagging along for the ride.

With best wishes,

Christy x

The Unforgettable Spanish Tycoon

—

Christy McKellen

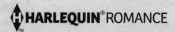

Recycling programs
for this product may
not exist in your area.

ISBN-13: 978-0-373-74421-3

The Unforgettable Spanish Tycoon

First North American Publication 2017

Copyright © 2017 by Christy McKellen

Printed in U.S.A.

www.Harlequin.com

Formerly a video and radio producer, **Christy McKellen** now spends her time writing fun, impassioned and emotive romance with an undercurrent of sensual tension. When she's not writing she can be found enjoying life with her husband and three children, walking for pleasure and researching other people's deepest secrets and desires. Christy loves to hear from readers. You can get hold of her at christymckellen.com.

Books by Christy McKellen

Harlequin Romance

Maids Under the Mistletoe

A Countess for Christmas

Unlocking Her Boss's Heart
One Week with the French Tycoon

Harlequin KISS

Holiday with a Stranger
Lessons in Rule-Breaking
Fired by Her Fling
Bridesmaid with Attitude

Visit the Author Profile page
at Harlequin.com for more titles.

This story is dedicated to my supersmart friend Erica, who talked me through the different types of amnesia and their symptoms, then patiently listened to my rambling and slightly bonkers story idea and still pronounced it something she'd love to read. I really appreciate the time you took to help me shape it into something workable. And thanks for always being such a good friend.

CHAPTER ONE

IT WAS UNSEASONABLY hot in Barcelona for February and, what with the adrenaline-spiked blood rushing through her veins and the brilliant sunshine that beat in waves at her back as she alighted from the cab outside Araya Industries' ultra-modern offices, Elena Jones was just about ready to combust in her made-for-English-weather woollen suit.

After giving her name in the wonderfully cool air-conditioned reception area, she was shown into a meeting room by a rather anxious-looking PA, acutely aware of the sound of her heels clicking loudly on the highly patterned ceramic tile flooring.

Swallowing down a twinge of nerves, Elena accepted the offer of a drink of water from the young woman, who for some reason didn't seem to be able to look her in the eye, then chose a chair at the head of the imposing twenty-seater frosted glass-topped table, carefully hanging her suit jacket over the back of the sharply stylish but rather uncomfortable-looking chair so it didn't get crumpled. She wanted to look her absolute best today in the hope it would provide her with the boost of confidence she needed to get a positive result from this meeting.

What was making her most nervous was not knowing how Caleb Araya was going to react to seeing her again after all this time. She was actually annoyed by just how anxious she felt about being out of her comfort zone. After running her own company for the last five years she'd become far better at taking risks and getting a grip on her fear of the unknown, and it took something rather exceptional to faze her now.

Apparently the thought of coming face-to-face with Caleb again was to be one of those things.

Would he have forgiven her by now?

Her heart gave an extra hard thump in her chest.

He had to have done, surely? What happened between them had been fifteen years ago; he couldn't still be holding a grudge. He was a businessman after all, a hugely successful one by all accounts, who wouldn't pass up the opportunity to get in on a profitable deal just because they had a bit of a rocky past.

Would he?

Staring out of the floor-to-ceiling windows at the busy street below, she remembered how she'd felt the very first time she'd met him during her second year at the University of Cambridge. At the tender age of twenty she'd thought Caleb Araya was the most arresting, ambitious and charismatic man she'd ever met.

They'd been good friends once, able to talk for hours about their passion for engineering and their hopes of making a mark on the world after they'd gained their degrees.

They'd made a strange pair, the two of them, so much so that their classmates had found their friendship a great source of amusement: she a petite, middle class, inner-city-living bookworm and he a hulking bad boy from the wrong side of a small Spanish town.

But away from other people the formerly

laconic, gruff Caleb had been playful, gentle and animated. He'd fascinated her with his passion and drive, not to mention his dangerous sex appeal, and had excited her in ways she'd never experienced before.

What she'd most loved about him was that despite having a tough start in life Caleb hadn't let it beat him down. He'd been determined to better his situation through sheer hard work and making intelligent decisions.

Looking around her now, she could see he'd certainly achieved his goal, and then some. According to the articles she'd read on the Web, his was now the most successful technology and engineering company ever to come out of Spain.

The door in the remarkably fingerprint-free wall of glass that divided the room from the large, plush reception area swung open, letting in the sound of Spanish chatter, and she stood up, taking a deep breath and preparing herself to face Caleb with a cool head and a warm smile.

She was determined not to let her shame about the heartless way she'd treated him in the past get in the way of her objective here today.

Hopefully, he wouldn't let any residual antipathy towards her get in the way of a promising business partnership either.

A wave of nervous tension made her skin prickle as the man himself strode into the room with his PA hot on his heels.

Caleb was just as captivating as she remembered, probably even more so now that he'd grown into his darkly arresting looks and six foot five, broad-shouldered frame. It seemed he'd only built on the animal magnetism she remembered so keenly too. With his dark, hooded eyes and jet-black hair slicked away from his strong-boned face he looked fierce, indomitable and rather dangerous.

No wonder his PA seemed so afraid of him.

The scowl currently marring his craggy features as he approached was so intimidating it made Elena's heart leap about in her chest.

'Elena Jones,' he drawled in that same beautiful gravelly Spanish accent she remembered so well, his voice sounding not so much friendly as vaguely amused.

Her stomach jumped with nerves as he came to a halt in front of where she stood.

Instead of holding out a hand in greeting, he folded his enormous arms, making his shirt sleeves tighten over his bulging muscles, and looked down at her with one dark eyebrow raised, as if waiting for her to explain how she could possibly have the nerve to show her face here.

He hadn't forgiven her then.

She swallowed hard, wishing she could take a quick sip of water to loosen her suddenly dry throat, but she didn't want to weaken her position by breaking eye contact with him so she ignored the impulse.

'It's good to see you again, Caleb. Thank you for agreeing to this meeting.'

His mouth twitched at the corner as if he were suppressing a smile. 'My former PA made it without my knowledge,' he said, glancing quickly towards his current PA, who seemed to shrink into herself a little, as if afraid she was about to take the fall for her predecessor's mistake. 'But when I saw your name in my diary I couldn't help but be curious about what you could possibly want from me after all this time.'

His presence seemed to grow, crowding out the light in the room as he dropped his arms and drew his shoulders back, pulling himself up to his full height. 'I'm guessing you're only here because you need something from me—rather desperately, judging by the power suit and heels.'

Damn, his dispassionate attitude was going to make her job here so much harder. But there was no way she was giving up that easily. Just because he wasn't prepared to be friendly it didn't mean she couldn't persuade him to agree to give her what she needed. She was going to have to play this meeting carefully though. Apologise— again—if that was what it took.

Just not yet.

It was probably best to keep things on a purely business tack for now.

'I'm here to put a proposition to you,' she said, forcing herself to keep her gaze firmly fixed to his. 'Although to say I'm "desperate" isn't at all accurate,' she lied.

If she knew Caleb at all, and she thought

that she did, showing any kind of weakness at this point would be a huge mistake.

'A proposition?' he said, a hint of incredulity colouring his voice.

Elena nodded jerkily, cursing her churning stomach. 'Yes. I'm sure it's something you're going to be very interested in.'

There was a heavy pause while Caleb ran his piercing gaze over her face—perhaps looking for signs of a set-up, or even a joke—before appearing to decide that she was absolutely serious.

'Then I suppose we'd better sit down,' he said, gesturing towards the chair she'd vacated and taking another one two places away, which he turned around so it was facing her.

'You won't need to take any notes,' he said to his PA, waving his hand dismissively. 'This won't be a long meeting.'

Trying not to show how much his glib assumption riled her, Elena took her own seat and smiled encouragingly at the PA, who gave her a nervous nod in return before scuttling out of the room.

Poor woman.

Biting her lip to refrain from saying something to Caleb about his ogre-like behaviour, Elena sat up straighter in her chair and fixed him with a serious stare.

He looked back at her with one eyebrow raised in apparent curiosity, though the look in his eyes was still hard enough to cut diamonds.

'I don't know whether you know, but I'm the Managing Director and owner of a company in England called Zipabout,' she began, leaning forward a little in her chair.

His expression gave no hint as to whether he'd known that or not so she decided to just forge ahead with the pitch.

'We've designed an electric car specifically suited for a single person to make short trips around towns and cities. It's safer than riding a bike and easy to park in small spaces, but the overarching benefits are that it'll help cut down on air pollution and unnecessary fuel usage.' She took a breath. 'Right now we're looking to source a large rechargeable battery to run it. The one that your company makes would be a perfect fit for our design.'

The smile he gave her made her think of a wild animal about to pounce.

'You're asking me to partner with you?' he asked with dry amusement in his voice.

She cleared her throat to try and defuse the tension that was building there.

'That's exactly what I'm proposing.'

He nodded slowly, his intense gaze never leaving her face.

'Why did you choose my battery?'

'It's the best one on the market.' She held back on revealing that it was the *only* one that would work with the design now that their previous choice was no longer viable.

When their former supplier had called a meeting at the eleventh hour to let her know there was an unfixable fault with the battery they'd planned to use in the car, Elena had done some frantic research, only to come to the uncomfortable conclusion that Caleb's company was the only other manufacturer of a battery compatible with the design. If she didn't get him to agree to supply her company today it was quite likely the car's product launch would be perilously held up and they'd lose all the pre-orders they'd worked so hard to accrue.

'And I think a partnership would be highly beneficial for both our companies,' she went on, hoping to goodness that her nerves weren't beginning to show. Her whole body was rigid with tension because, most crucially, if he didn't agree to supply the battery Zipabout could go under and her entire workforce, who had become like family to her over the last five years, would all lose their jobs.

Tamping down on the dread that sank through her at the thought of it, she widened her smile. 'I sent some information over to your PA this morning in case you had a chance to look at it before the meeting, but I'm guessing from your reaction that you haven't. I have a short presentation on my laptop with me though; perhaps you'd like to see it?'

He regarded her without speaking for what felt like minutes, his dark eyes narrowed in thought. There was something else there in his expression that she didn't like the look of. Something cold and hard.

'No, I don't think I would,' he said finally.

She stared at him, wondering whether she'd misheard. Surely he couldn't be dismissing the idea without at least looking at her proposal?

'What—?' she whispered, giving herself a little shake, then leaning in closer to him. 'Caleb, at least look at the sales projections—'

But he cut her off with a wave of his hand. 'I'm not interested in partnering with you, Elena.' He stood up. 'Now, if you'll excuse me, I have a busy day—'

'Wait!' She raised her hand with all but her pointing finger clenched into a fist so he wouldn't see how sweaty her palm was. 'I haven't given you all the salient details yet,' she said desperately.

'I don't need to hear them; I've already made my decision.'

'But—' She could feel panic rising from her gut. 'Why, Caleb?'

He took a step towards her, his face completely devoid of emotion. 'Because, Elena, I don't do business with people whose word I don't trust.'

She shook her head in disbelief. 'That was a long time ago, Caleb. I can't believe you're still angry with me for that.' Getting shakily to her feet, she took a step towards him. 'Please know I still feel bad about the way I handled it all, but we were both so young and naïve—'

'You were naïve,' he cut in angrily. 'I wasn't. I'd experienced far too much ignorance and cruelty in my life for that to be the case.'

'And you're really still harbouring bad feelings about it? It was fifteen years ago! Surely you've experienced enough happiness in your life now to get over it?' She swallowed down her regret. 'I read that you got engaged last year.'

He batted away her questioning look, his gaze finally slipping from hers. 'It didn't work out.'

Something twisted and tightened in her chest, making it harder for her to breathe. 'I'm sorry to hear that.'

His expression darkened. 'Are you? Since when do you care about my love life?'

'I—' She didn't know how to answer that. The truth was she'd kept tabs on what he'd been up to over the intervening years because, despite the fact their friendship had ended badly, she still cared about him. Not that she thought telling him that right now would do anything to strengthen her case. He'd probably just see it as more weakness.

Caleb used her hesitation to push the knife in deeper.

'How *is*—what was his name?—Johnny, was it? Are the two of you still living your safe, comfortable life together?'

Heat raced to her cheeks. 'His name was Jimmy and, no, we're not together any more. We split up a number of years ago.' Which was yet another painful regret. She still felt guilty about backing away from her and Jimmy's wedding, even though she'd known it was the right thing to do at the time.

The main problem had been that the memories of Caleb had never left her, even though she'd tried her hardest to forget him. He'd stayed with her, buried deep in her heart.

There wasn't a flicker of reaction on Caleb's face at this news though, not even a twitch of an eye. Clearly he didn't care a jot about her any more. But then, if that was true, why was he being so pig-headed about not listening to her?

Because he was punishing her for hurting him *fifteen* years ago.

Frustration surged through her. 'I can't believe you're still holding a grudge, Caleb. Surely someone of your standing and success has no need to be so small-minded.' She could hear the anger vibrating in her voice and it seemed Caleb did too because he widened his eyes a little before replacing his flash of surprise with an amused smirk.

'Is this the controlled, cautious Elena I knew all those years ago? My, how you've changed.'

'For the better, Caleb. I'm not the naïve young girl you used to know.' She refrained from saying *and love*, knowing that would be taking things a step too far. He'd never said such a thing to her, he'd been too proud for that, though it had been implied in his every action.

Unless she'd read him wrongly.

Which was quite possible.

She'd been wrong about a lot of things.

There was a quiet knock on the glass door and Caleb's PA crept, hunch-shouldered, into the room.

Before she could speak, Caleb let out a growl of frustration and snapped, 'I thought I told you I didn't want to be interrupted!'

Because Caleb had spoken to her in English, and perhaps in deference to Elena's presence there too, his PA replied in English. 'I'm so sorry, but I thought you'd want to know about this straight away. Apparently there's a problem with the meeting with the Americans on Monday. Señor Carter's PA is saying he's having second thoughts—'

Caleb held up a hand to stop her speaking, his gaze flicking momentarily to Elena before returning to his PA, his expression thunderous, as if furious that Elena had been a party to hearing about the setback.

This time he replied in Spanish and, even though Elena didn't understand a word of it, not being a Spanish speaker, she could see that his words had cut his PA deeply when she backed out of the room with tears glinting in her eyes.

'How can you be so cold? So *mean*!' she blurted when he turned back to look at her. 'That poor woman was just doing her job.'

Mouth dry, she reached for the glass of water but when she saw how much her hand was trembling she quickly dropped it to her side again.

'How could you treat her like that, Caleb?'

'Like what?' he growled.

'Like nothing. Less than nothing. I would have thought you'd have made every effort to make sure your subordinates were treated with kindness and respect after what you went through when you were young.'

Anger flickered in his eyes. 'I'm respectful to people when they work hard and make good choices.'

'But people won't learn from their mistakes if you don't nurture them. They become afraid to take necessary risks and everything grinds to a halt.'

'Is that what's happened to your business, Elena?' he asked quietly. 'Did you drive it into the ground with your inept handling of your staff so you were forced to come here, begging for my help? What a fall from grace that must be for you.'

Hot rage rushed through her body. How could the smart, compassionate man she remembered have become so hard and mean? 'I knew you could be a bit on the curt side, Caleb, but the man I knew was never cruel. Or a bully!'

Shock flashed momentarily across his

face before it was replaced with a stony scowl. 'Enough! This meeting is over. I don't need you coming in here, telling me how to treat my staff. Go home and run your own business—' he leant in closer to her so she saw the conviction plainly in his eyes '—without my battery.'

With that closing shot, he turned his back on her and strode out of the room, leaving the glass door swinging in his wake.

Caleb Araya paced the floor of his corner office, his blood pumping frantically through his veins.

Who did Elena Jones think she was, turning up after fifteen years of silence and presuming to tell him how to run his business and treat his staff?

The woman certainly had some nerve.

And a skewed sense of priorities.

Not that he didn't already know that from experience.

To his utter frustration, and despite the fact they hadn't seen each other in a very long time, as soon as he'd seen her standing there in his meeting room he'd been hit hard by that same immediate connection they'd always shared.

It had put him on the back foot.

It had always been like that with her—she affected him like no other woman ever had. The moment he'd met her at the beginning of his Erasmus exchange year to the University of Cambridge he'd found himself drawn to her.

Her cool integrity and assertive sense of self had set her apart from the other immature, entitled female students that had swarmed around him, believing him to be an ideal candidate for the bad boy fling they were so keen to tick off their list before settling down with their rich, boring husbands.

They hadn't bothered to get to know *him* at all.

Elena, on the other hand, had made him feel as if he didn't need to pretend to be somebody he wasn't when he was with her. She'd liked him for his erudite conversation and refreshing views on the world. Or so she'd said.

After growing up as the poor, pitied son of a woman who was infamous in the small town where he lived for being the mistress of a married man and a woman of loose morals, he'd promised himself he'd make sure his adulthood would be very different.

Because of the disgrace that surrounded his family, his early life had been pretty tough by all accounts: friendless, violent and isolated. But after he'd been threatened with expulsion from the elite school that he'd later found, to his chagrin, that his mother's sugar daddy had funded, he'd pulled up his socks and eschewed everything and everyone for a life dedicated to study so he could get away from the small town and its even smaller mentality.

He was going to be someone that people looked up to and respected, and Elena had made him feel as though he'd achieved that—for a short time anyway.

To his shame and regret, it had turned out he'd been very wrong about how much she'd actually cared about him and she'd been the first and last person he'd ever trusted.

The memory of her betrayal had stayed with him over the years, tarnishing every relationship he'd had, as if she were a devil on his shoulder, judging his choices, prodding at his conscience, reminding him he could never truly trust anyone with his heart.

When he'd seen her name in his diary this morning it had sent a shock of such intense regret-fuelled nostalgia through him he'd had to sit down and take a few deep breaths to regain his composure. He'd been on the cusp of telling his PA to cancel the meeting, but curiosity and a deep-seated urge to regain some sort of equilibrium over past hurts had stopped him at the last minute.

He wanted to feel as though he finally had a handle on his feelings about Elena Jones.

It had been going well, with him feeling in control of the meeting until she'd caught him out by accusing him of being a bully.

It had shocked him to his core.

Was that really what she thought he'd become?

It had been such a long time since someone had stood up to him like that, he had no idea whether his behaviour was out of line or not. The thought that it might have been had rattled him. *She'd* rattled him, despite his determination not to let her get to him.

He stabbed at the buzzer on the phone to summon his PA.

Benita hurried into the room, her hands

tightly clasped in front of her and her gaze lowered as if she was afraid she'd get another dressing-down for what had just happened.

He'd been furious when she'd let it slip in front of Elena that things weren't exactly going to plan with the Americans. He'd not wanted her to know that things weren't running as smoothly as he'd wanted to project, for the sake of his professional pride, but he was aware, now that he'd calmed down a little, that he'd perhaps been a bit too harsh on the woman. She'd not been working for him for long, having stepped into the role after his usual PA had gone on maternity leave, and they hadn't found the right rhythm for working together yet.

But he wasn't a complete monster, as Elena had so brazenly suggested. He was firm and expected total professionalism at all times, but he made sure to reward those who did a good job for him.

'Benita, I wanted to say good work on putting that file together for me yesterday. It was very helpful in my meeting.'

His PA stared at him, as if in shock.

Surely it wasn't that surprising that he'd offered her a compliment.

Was it?

No. He was letting Elena Jones get into his head and that was the last place he wanted her to be. He was over his feelings for her. It had taken him years to get rid of the ache he'd carried around after she'd rejected him, but he'd finally managed it.

'Thank you.' Benita paused, a worried frown now pinching her brow. 'Are you okay? Is there anything I can get you?' she asked with hesitation in her voice.

He opened his mouth to dismiss her misplaced concern, annoyed that she'd noticed his agitation, but pulled himself back at the last second, now hyper-aware of Elena's comments.

Damn the woman!

'I'm fine,' he muttered, forcing his mouth into a smile.

But, instead of seeming reassured by this, his PA took a hurried step away from him as if suspicious about his sudden change in attitude.

He sighed and ran a hand through his hair,

pacing to the window to look down at the street below and collect himself.

What was happening to him today? His head was a mess.

At least he was free of Elena now though. His outright rejection of her proposal would surely mean she'd never darken his door again.

The street was busy with people milling about between office blocks and cafés and he watched them scurrying around for a moment, his thoughts jumping between relief and dissatisfaction. He knew he'd been petty, not even agreeing to look at the proposal she'd brought all the way from England, but she'd humiliated and hurt him once and he wasn't prepared to let her get anywhere near him again.

A partnership between them—their *companies*, he corrected himself—could never work.

For a second he wondered whether his mind was playing tricks on him as a familiar lone figure on the street opposite his building caught his eye. His stomach lurched as he watched her pace back and forth, then throw her gaze up towards Araya

Industries and frown, as if hatching a plan to get back in here and torment him again.

Apparently he couldn't have been more wrong about having chased Elena Jones away for good.

Well, he wasn't having it.

'Hold my calls for a while longer,' he said to his PA as he swept out of the room past her and headed towards the lift that would take him down to street level.

Apparently he hadn't made it clear enough to Elena that there would be no further opportunities to meet with him, so he was going to rectify that right here and now. He was going to tell her to go home and that he wanted nothing more to do with her.

Storming onto the street, blood pulsing feverishly through his veins, he called out her name and she turned to meet his eye, her expression registering first surprise then hope.

Hope away, cariño—*you're not getting a thing from me except a wave goodbye.*

The street was quiet as he drew level with where she stood on the pavement opposite and he glanced quickly left, not seeing anything coming his way, anger at her audacity buzzing in his head.

Elena's eyes were fixed firmly on him as he began to cross the street towards her but, as he stepped into the middle of the road, something made her glance away then quickly back to him again.

This time there was an altogether different expression on her face.

Panic.

Blood thumping in his ears, he swivelled to look at what had spooked her and time seemed to slow down. There was a motorbike coming towards him at speed and he knew in that moment, with absolute certainty, that there was no way he could get out of its path in time.

Memories flashed before his eyes: of him and Elena laughing together after one of their classes at university, of her sitting in his room telling him she was thinking about splitting up with her childhood sweetheart, and all the blood rushing from his head as he realised he finally had a chance to have what he'd wanted for so long, of the look of abject hurt and distress on her face just now when he'd told her he wouldn't partner with her.

Lights and colours danced before his eyes

and a strange kind of euphoria lifted his senses, making his surroundings hyper-loud and vividly real.

And then the bike hit him, the impact throwing his body into the air, knocking all the breath from his lungs. In a panic he flailed his limbs wildly as he tried to grab hold of something, anything, to anchor him as he spun through the void. A moment later his body made rough, painful impact with the ground, quickly followed by his head.

And everything went black.

CHAPTER TWO

ELENA STOOD IN SHOCK, her arms still out-stretched as if she'd thought she could do something, some kind of magic perhaps, to stop Caleb from being hit by the motorbike that had sped round the corner just as he'd stepped into its path.

She felt light-headed and displaced from reality, as if this was all some horrible dream—though the heavy thump of her heart in her throat and the adrenaline that roared through her body told her otherwise.

The rider was picking himself up from the ground after coming off his bike and miraculously seemed not to be injured in any way, but Caleb's slumped body, which had been flung at least ten feet, was still lying half on the pavement and half on the road. And he wasn't moving.

A cacophony of noise suddenly rushed

in on her as people began running towards where Caleb lay, finally shocking Elena out of her dazed state. She stumbled towards him, falling to her knees by his side, barely registering the rough ground biting into her skin, and put her shaking hand onto his torso. His eyes were closed, but she could feel his chest rising and falling with his breathing.

So he was still alive. *Thank God.*

She could feel tears pressing at the back of her eyes but she blinked them away, determined to keep it together for his sake.

'Caleb? Can you hear me?' she whispered, leaning in closer to him and breathing in the distinctive scent of him that had haunted her throughout the years, usually at the most inopportune moments.

Somebody—a woman—asked her a question in Spanish and Elena shook her head, mouthing back ineffectually, totally unable to summon even the basic Spanish phrase for *I don't understand*.

The woman frowned, then asked, 'Are you English?'

Was it that obvious?

Judging by the fact she was wearing a highly inappropriate woollen suit for the weather and had skin so light it was almost translucent, she guessed it must be.

'Yes!' Elena said, relief flooding through her that the woman would be able to help her. 'I don't speak Spanish.' She swallowed hard. 'I need to call an ambulance. Can you help me?'

'Don't worry,' the woman said, gesturing behind her. 'My husband has already called them.'

Caleb let out a low groan and Elena swivelled back to look at him, her heart leaping with relief. 'Caleb? Are you okay? I'm so sorry—this is all my fault.'

At least it felt like it was her fault, even though rationally she knew it had been an accident. But it was also another thing for him to hold against her.

She should have left this area and gone to regroup somewhere else—to give Caleb a chance to calm down—then come back again once her head was clear and her plan fully formed, instead of pacing about in front of his building like a lunatic. He must have seen her prowling around out here and decided to come out to ask her what the hell she thought she was doing.

When she'd heard him call her name from across the street her first thought had been that he'd changed his mind and decided to listen to her after all and her heart had leapt with excitement and relief. But as he'd crossed the street and she'd seen the look of frustrated fury in his eyes it had become powerfully obvious that she'd been very wrong to suppose that.

He hadn't wanted to turn back the clock. He'd wanted her gone.

The woman laid a hand gently onto her back, dragging her out of her distraught reflection. 'He'll be okay, don't worry. The ambulance is on its way.'

Elena nodded gratefully, this time unable to stop tears from welling in her eyes. 'He was crossing the road to meet me and didn't see the bike.'

'It's okay. Not your fault,' the woman said in a soothing tone, rubbing Elena's arm in sympathy.

If only that were true. She already felt guilty enough about the anguish she'd caused Caleb in the past and now she'd hurt him again, only physically this time. He never would have been out here if it wasn't for her.

A moment later the sound of a siren broke through the low murmurs of the crowd that had gathered around them and an ambulance sped round the corner and parked up nearby, its flashing lights bouncing off the windows of the buildings opposite.

The paramedics jumped out of the cab and ran towards where Caleb lay, pushing their way through the large group of bystanders that had gathered to ogle the drama playing out in front of them.

The helpful woman disappeared from Elena's side as the paramedics came to kneel next to Caleb and check his vital signs. The female paramedic turned to ask Elena a question in Spanish, indicating towards Caleb, and Elena guessed she must be asking whether she knew him.

Novia meant friend, didn't it? It sounded like a friendly kind of word.

'*Sí, sí!*' she said, her voice sounding shaky and weak from shock. The woman nodded and gave her a reassuring smile, then turned back to help her colleague tend to the now silent and deathly still Caleb.

A short while later he was lifted onto a

stretcher wearing a neck brace, then into the back of the ambulance.

Elena stood there stupidly, watching as they secured the straps to keep the make-shift bed from rolling around in the back of the vehicle, her chest tight with worry.

What if he died?

No. She couldn't think like that. He'd be fine. The paramedics weren't rushing around shouting and wielding scary-looking equipment as if they were worried that he was in grave danger. Mercifully, there was hardly any blood on the ground where he'd lain, just a little from where he'd cut his temple.

Perhaps he'd just been knocked out and not badly hurt. Just a bit bruised and battered.

Please.

Please.

Elena didn't realise the female paramedic had said something to her until the woman waved a hand in front of her face and spoke again, her expression registering sympathy. 'You come. To hospital.'

Elena nodded dumbly, not entirely sure it was appropriate that she should be the one to go with Caleb, but no one from his company had rushed out to be here with him. It looked as though the paramedics wanted to get him straight to hospital now so there wasn't time to go into his building and find someone.

She should just go with him and call his office from there to let them know what was going on. Then she'd leave him be and go back to the hotel to get her head together.

One thing was for sure, going to pieces was not going to help anyone right now.

Mind made up, she gave the paramedic a wobbly smile and climbed into the back of the ambulance.

There was something wrong with the light in his bedroom, Caleb thought fuzzily as he woke up from a deep, dreamless sleep. And his cleaning lady seemed to have used a different kind of product than usual because he didn't recognise the smell in here either.

'Ah, you're awake,' came a voice from somewhere to his left and he wondered wildly who he'd gone to bed with the night before.

He couldn't remember.

In fact, now he thought about it, he found his mind was strangely blank, as if it had been wiped of details. How much had he drunk last night to wake up in this state? It must have been a lot because he had the unsettling feeling that he wasn't at home at all. In fact, he realised with a lurch as his vision cleared, he had no idea where he was or how he'd got here. The walls were painted an institutional green colour and were disturbingly free of any kind of decoration. Turning his head, he saw with a shock that he was lying next to some kind of flashing, beeping, monitoring machine with wires and drips hanging from it.

Which were attached to him.

He tried to sit up and felt his whole body complain, pain shooting through his abdomen.

'No, no, don't try and get up. You had an accident and you've cracked a rib and banged your head so you may feel dizzy and disorientated for a while.'

'An accident?' he asked, shocked by how rough and raspy his voice sounded. His throat was so dry it felt as if he hadn't had a drink in days.

'Here,' the voice said and he turned towards where it came from to see a middle-aged woman in a crisp white uniform standing next to the bed where he lay, pushing a straw towards his mouth.

He sipped gratefully from the drink, feeling the cool liquid soothe his throat and begin to refresh him.

'Your girlfriend's very worried about you,' the nurse said, taking the cup away once he'd finished and putting it on the nightstand next to his bed. 'She saw you get hit by the motorbike and is blaming herself for the accident because you were crossing the road to see her when it happened, so be nice to her when she comes in to see you.'

'My girlfriend?' He didn't remember having a girlfriend.

His heart began to race as panic swept through him, nausea welling in his stomach as the room started to slowly spin. He shook his head, trying to clear the feeling, determined not to give in to it.

He didn't do panic, dammit.

Not appearing to notice his disorientation, the nurse helped him sit up a little so she could fluff up his pillow and he gripped the rail at the side of the bed hard, racking his brain for the memory of how he came to be here in an attempt to centre himself. The nurse had said a motorbike had hit him but he had absolutely no recollection of it.

How could he not remember something so serious?

'I think she needs a hug and some reassurance that you don't hate her,' she said, smiling at him. 'Judging by the way she's been pacing the halls and badgering us every ten minutes for updates on your condition, she obviously cares about you very much. You're a lucky man to have someone who loves you like that.'

He just nodded, not wanting to let on that he had no idea who she was talking about, or that he was becoming more and more aware of other rather worrying gaps in his memory. He knew his name and that he owned a company called Araya Industries, which he'd built up from scratch, and that he lived in the L'Eixample district of Barcelona. He even knew what the inside of his penthouse looked like, but things like where he grew up and who his friends were seemed to have escaped him. And he definitely didn't remember being hit by the motorbike. The last thing he did remember was getting into work this morning and turning on his computer, but after that it was all a blank.

This disjoin in his memory made him feel sick if he thought about it too much, so he decided to put it out of his head for now. It would all come back after he'd been awake for a while and had got his bearings again. And he didn't want any fuss; he just wanted to get out of here, back to his home. Maybe once in familiar surroundings his mind would catch up with everything else.

'I'll let her know you're awake so she can come in and see you,' the nurse said, coming over to him and smoothing down the sheet that was covering him up to his armpits. It seemed they'd stripped him of the rest of his clothes, perhaps to check him over for injuries.

'Who?' he asked distractedly, still trying to get a handle on the anxiety that stubbornly surged through his body.

'Your girlfriend, Elena.' The nurse frowned, as if beginning to suspect that all was not entirely well with him.

He shot her a quick smile and said, 'Okay, good, I'd like to see her.'

Perhaps as soon as he saw this Elena he'd recognise her right away and the rest of his memory would come flooding back with it.

The nurse nodded curtly, clearly still a little suspicious about his well-being, but then turned and left the room.

A moment later there was a tentative knock at the door. He sat up a little straighter in bed and called, 'Come in.'

A woman with ice-blue eyes and long blonde hair hanging loosely around her slim shoulders entered the room and walked towards him, coming to a stop a couple of feet away from the bed. Her movements appeared graceful and controlled, but he could see from her strained smile that she was tense and worried.

Something about her shot a bolt of intense sensation through him, almost like déjà vu, though he could have sworn he'd never set eyes on her before in his life. He had vague memories of relationships with other women, beautiful, smart women, but there was something about Elena, something almost untouchable, that unnerved him. Or was that just his addled brain playing tricks on him? He'd obviously banged his head pretty hard if he'd forgotten he was having a relationship with a woman as attractive as this.

'How are you feeling?' she asked in English, which for some reason seemed absolutely right and totally expected.

'I'm okay—a bit banged up, but I'll live,' he said, patting a space on the bed next to him, wanting her to come nearer so he could study her closer. He had the strangest feeling that if he touched her he'd feel more grounded.

She looked at him warily for a moment then visibly swallowed before stepping up to perch on the edge of the mattress, as if worried about getting too close and knocking him and causing him pain.

Desire shot through him as the scent of her perfume hit his senses and he closed his eyes for a moment, feeling another wave of déjà vu sweep through him.

Come on brain, catch up.

'It's good to see you awake. I was really worried about you,' she said, her voice sounding a little croaky.

'You're trembling,' he murmured, reaching out to touch her arm, feeling her practically vibrating under his fingertips.

'I wasn't sure what to expect when I came in here,' she said, her gaze darting away from his face to look down at where his tanned hand rested on her pale skin.

'Well, you don't need to worry. I'm fine,' he stated vehemently, hoping to reassure her—and perhaps himself a little too—though, judging by the tremble in her bottom lip, it didn't appear to have worked.

He *was* fine though, he told himself hazily, just a bit disorientated…that was all. Just because the sight of her hadn't brought his memory back, it didn't mean it was gone for good.

Perhaps if he kissed her, it would spark something in his brain.

She certainly looked as though she could do with some proof that he was still the man she knew and cared about. What was it the nurse had said? That she blamed herself for the accident because he'd been crossing the road to see her at the time? Was that the problem here—was she worried he was angry with her?

'Come closer,' he said, moving his hand up to slide his fingers under her jaw, feeling a strong urge to wipe the concern from her beautiful face now.

She stilled under his touch and her eyes widened as if she was surprised by what he was doing.

'Stop worrying,' he murmured, then drew her towards him and pressed his mouth firmly to hers.

She sucked in a startled-sounding breath but he paid it no mind, pulling her closer to him, ignoring the twinge of pain this caused in his damaged rib and hoping against hope that this would make everything right again.

Her mouth felt wonderful against his but he was blurrily aware that the kiss wasn't having the effect he'd hoped for. Determined not to give up that easily, he opened his lips and slipped his tongue into the heat of her mouth. As he'd suspected, she tasted incredible, like honey and harmony and sex...

And then his brain seemed to switch gear and suddenly he couldn't get enough of her. It was like having that first drink of water all over again, his body reacting with a forceful relief that shook him to his very soul. Her full mouth was soft but not as pliant as he would have liked, so he kissed her harder, feeling the pulse in her neck racing against the heel of his hand where he cupped her jaw.

A deep growl rumbled in the back of his throat as he began to lose control of his restraint and she let out a breathy moan in reply and dug her nails into the flesh of his upper arms.

He sank into the possessiveness of her grip, lost in the sensual taste of her, feeling the strangest mixture of comfort and desire and relief—until he suddenly became aware that she was trying to pull away from him.

Reluctantly, he slid his hands away from her jaw and let her go.

'What's wrong?' he ground out, frustrated that she'd cut the kiss short when he'd been enjoying it so much.

It had been the first time he'd felt anything like himself since he'd woken up here.

Her eyes were wide and her expression a little wild. 'Why did you kiss me?' Almost absent-mindedly, she brushed her fingers against her lips and his body reacted with such erotic force he very nearly dragged her back to him again for another round.

But the look in her eyes stopped him.

He could see now that she was shaken by the kiss and not because she'd enjoyed it as much as he had.

'Why shouldn't I kiss you?' he demanded, feeling panic begin to work its way back under his skin again.

She blinked at him, looking utterly bewildered, her cheeks flushed with colour and her brow creased. 'Because of what happened this morning. We had a row.'

He frowned, his mind spinning with confusion. 'You mean before the accident? Look, I'm sure that wasn't your fault; I can't have been looking where I was going.'

Getting up from the bed, she took a step away from him, crossing her arms and frowning hard as if she didn't understand what she was hearing. 'Caleb, don't you remember what happened?'

He wanted to say yes, that he remembered everything, but he knew, with a slow sinking feeling of dread, that there was actually something very, very wrong here.

Throwing up his hands in frustration, he said, 'No! Okay! I don't remember!'

She flinched in surprise, then stared at him in horror, her mouth forming a perfect O shape.

Closing his eyes, he attempted to pull his focus back and took a long, deep breath. Fighting to keep his voice steady this time, he said, 'The truth is my memory's been a little fuzzy since I woke up.' He ran a hand over his face then looked up at her. 'I don't remember anything between getting to work this morning and waking up in the hospital and anything before my life here in Barcelona is a little difficult to pin down—'

She was still staring at him in dismay. 'Oh, no, Caleb. That's not good.'

He flapped a hand dismissively, hating the idea of her pitying him. 'It's fine; it'll come back to me soon. It's probably just the drugs messing with my head.'

Taking a step closer to him, she said with a shake in her voice, 'Caleb, do you remember who I am?'

'Yes, you're Elena, my girlfriend,' he said airily, hoping it sounded more convincing to her than it did to him.

Her eyes grew comically wide. 'What makes you think I'm your girlfriend?'

Confusion swirled through his head again. 'Because…I thought…' He paused and frowned. 'The nurse told me you were, and I *know* I know you. You're very familiar to me.'

Elena shifted on the spot, looking uncomfortable now. 'I don't speak Spanish so I must have misinterpreted the paramedic's question when she asked me about my relationship to you,' she muttered to herself, staring down at the floor. 'Or perhaps the nurse got the wrong end of the stick or something.' She looked up at him again, her brow pinched into a frown. 'Anyway, however it happened, I'm not your girlfriend.'

He looked at her for a moment and got the distinct impression there was more to this than she was telling him.

'So we're what?' he asked slowly, one eyebrow raised. 'Just friends?'

Elena knew that lying to Caleb was the last thing she should do right now but she didn't want to add any unnecessary stress to the situation, not when he'd only just woken up from an accident with a head injury and seemed to be rather confused.

And the thing was, they *had* been friends once, very good friends, and if she had any say in the matter she'd make sure they got past their differences to become friends again.

But that would be all. Just friends.

Even though the kiss they'd just shared had rocked her world. Her whole body still buzzed from the after-effects of the feel of his firm mouth on hers—her pulse jumping in her throat and her nerves on fire with a wild, almost frightening demand for more that she'd not felt the like of in years.

Not since the last time he'd kissed her.

'Uh-huh. We haven't seen each other for a long time though. We knew each other at university.' She waited for him to recall the fact that they weren't exactly friends any more but his expression remained blank. It seemed he really didn't remember her.

'I'm just visiting from England for a few days and dropped in to see you,' she added, wondering if that would help jog his memory, but it didn't appear to. He was looking at her with such an intense expression in his eyes now, as if he was thinking about kissing her again, that she had to drag her gaze away and look down instead at the sheet that was tucked up against his rather impressive bare chest. She tried not to stare too hard at it, or at the dark bruises marking his skin. Apart from those, he was in really good shape, his limbs strong and muscled, his torso toned and hard.

Stop gawping, you fool!

'I'm sorry if I've made you feel awkward,' Caleb said, frowning and shaking his head, then closing one eye and squinting as if the movement had caused him great pain.

She went to put out a hand to touch him, then withdrew it. 'Is your head hurting?'

'Like crazy.'

'I'll get the doctor.'

She started to walk away, then paused and turned back to face him. 'Is there someone else you want me to call to be here with you?'

He looked at her in surprise, before frowning. 'No, I don't think so. To be honest, I can't think of who I would call.' He looked so uncomfortable she couldn't help but feel a rush of sympathy for him.

She was just about to offer to stay until they were able to contact a friend in Barcelona for him when his expression cleared and he said, 'Could you ring my office and ask my PA to come here?'

'I've already called her,' she told him. 'She's on her way over. I asked her who your emergency contact is but she wasn't sure. Apparently she hasn't been working for you for long.'

'No. My regular PA has just had a baby.'

'It's not yours, is it?' she quipped, then regretted it when she saw a look of panic flash across his face.

'I'm just joking, Caleb. Sorry, that was tasteless of me considering your state of mind at the moment.' She squeezed her eyes shut and wrinkled her nose. 'I'm still a little shaken up after what just happened.'

But, instead of giving her a piece of his mind, he gave her a slow, wry smile instead, like the ones he used to give her back when they were friends. It was such an incredible sight and something she'd not seen for such a long time it stopped her in her tracks.

'I'll…er…go and find a doctor,' she said

hurriedly, swallowing down the lump that had formed in her throat.

Turning away, she strode out of the room on rather shaky legs, relieved to be able to get away from his befuddling presence for a moment so she could figure out how the heck she was going to handle this situation from this point on.

Just as she reached the nurses' station Caleb's PA hurried around the corner and, spotting her, gave a little wave of recognition.

'Benita, thank you for coming,' Elena said as the woman came to a breathless halt in front of her. 'Caleb's okay, but he's banged his head and is having trouble remembering which friend to call to come and look after him. Has he mentioned anyone to you that he's close to?' she asked.

Benita shook her head, biting her lip and looking a little anxious. 'I've only been working for him for a few days and he never talks about anything of a personal nature. I checked his computer and his work mobile—which he'd left on his desk,' she added a little defensively, as if Elena might accuse her of snooping, 'but there was no one obvious I should call.'

Turning away, she began rifling through her bag, her movements becoming increasingly desperate as she failed to locate what she was looking for. '*Caramba!* I forgot to put his phone in here.'

Elena put a steadying hand onto the woman's arm. 'It's okay. He's in no state to be using his phone right now anyway. In fact, it's probably better if he doesn't have it right away. Less stress.'

She nodded, though the expression in her eyes reflected her worry. 'I'll drop it round to his apartment later.'

'I'm sure that would be fine,' Elena said in an attempt to soothe the poor woman.

Sighing, Benita shook her head. 'Carla would never have forgotten it.'

That gave Elena an idea. 'Hey, would Carla know of a friend of his to contact?' she asked hopefully.

Benita shook her head again. 'I called her but she said the same thing. He never gave away much personal information about himself. He had a few girlfriends over the time she worked for him but she never met any of them and he's not seeing anyone now, as far as she knows. He doesn't have any family left either, now his mother's passed away.'

Elena experienced a pang of sorrow on his behalf. She knew from their time at university that he'd always been a bit of a loner and that his mother had been his only family, not that they'd been particularly close. He'd been angry with her for continuing to have a long-term relationship with a married man. He didn't know who his father was either; his mother had refused to tell him, saying he was just a man she'd met in a bar one night. Unfortunately for Caleb, that had been a well chewed over piece of gossip in the town where he'd grown up, which had followed him round like a bad smell.

It was really no wonder he was so keen to keep his private life private these days.

'When did his mother pass away?' she asked.

'About six months ago, I think. Carla mentioned something about it because he'd actually taken some time off work for once to be with her in the hospice. It was cancer, apparently, that took her.'

The two women stood quietly for a moment, reflecting on this.

'Well, I'd better get back to the office now I know he's okay,' Benita said suddenly, smiling, as if Elena's presence there had released her from her own duties to Caleb. 'I'll let the other managers know what's happened and that he won't be in work for the rest of the week. Please tell him everything's under control. I know he'll worry otherwise.'

'Don't you want to go in and see him?' Elena asked, a little shocked by the woman's intention to withdraw without even saying hello to Caleb.

Benita shook her head, taking a step backwards. 'No, no. Just tell him I hope he feels better soon.'

'Well, perhaps someone else from work could come over and sort out who can look after him—' Elena said rather desperately, but Benita was backing away now, clearly keen to get out of there and return to the sanctuary of a Caleb-free office.

'I doubt anyone there will know any more than me,' she said, giving one last tight smile, then turning and rushing away.

Sighing, Elena rubbed a hand over her face, her insides sinking with a mixture of sadness for Caleb at his apparent lack of close friendships and nerves about exactly what she'd got herself into here.

The sad fact was, it looked as though the only person available to take care of him right now was her.

As she thought about this a crazy idea began to form in her head and her stomach gave a nervous little flip. Maybe if she could show him she was happy to be here for him, and prepared to help in any way she could, it might go some way towards rebuilding their friendship—without the prejudice and anger he seemed to be holding on to from the past getting in the way—and help her reconnect with the man she knew was in there, hiding behind that hard shell she'd seen earlier. Otherwise, once his memory came back she might never have the opportunity to speak to him again, especially when he remembered why he'd been crossing that road, but if she could be a good friend to him now and prove how much she cared about him, perhaps he'd think twice before pushing her away again.

It was worth a try.

Anything was worth a try at this point.

But if she did stay to look after him there would be no more kissing, she told herself firmly, setting back her shoulders and heading towards the desk to ask the staff there to contact his doctor.

Definitely not.

CHAPTER THREE

THE MEMORY OF Elena's captivating ice-blue eyes and her long slender legs with their dirty, scuffed up knees remained stubbornly imprinted in Caleb's mind as he lay back in bed and waited impatiently for her to return.

Just friends, huh? What on earth had stopped him from pursuing more than friendship with her? He'd very much like to know that. He found her intensely attractive and she was clearly a smart, compassionate person—qualities he valued highly.

An English rose.

The phrase floated into his mind. Yes, that summed her up perfectly.

A moment later the door opened and she strode back into the room with a tall dark-haired woman following closely behind her.

'Sorry I was away for so long; I bumped into your PA out there—she said to tell you she hopes you feel better soon and that she's got everything under control at work so you can rest without worrying—and then it took me a while to locate your doctor.' She gestured towards the woman she'd entered with.

'Señor Araya,' the doctor said, walking over to his bed and picking up the clipboard that hung at the end of it, 'how are you feeling?' She scanned the paperwork quickly before replacing the clipboard.

'I feel fine,' he said confidently. He didn't want to give her any reason to keep him here unnecessarily. He was uncomfortable with being in hospital; it made him feel vulnerable and edgy for some reason. He'd be much better off in his own home with his things around him. Maybe then his memory would come back.

The doctor pressed her lips together. 'So it seems you have a cracked rib and a bump on your head, but apart from that you got off pretty lightly, considering you were hit by a motorbike travelling at speed.'

'Can you speak English so Elena can understand?' he snapped, riled by the doctor's officious manner and not wanting Elena to feel ignored when she'd been good enough to stay and check on him. Unlike his PA.

'Yes, of course,' the doctor said, switching easily to English and giving Elena an indulgent smile before turning back to fix her scrutinising gaze on him again.

'I'd like you to stay here tonight. Head injuries can be serious and I'd like to keep you under observation for a while longer to make sure you're okay.'

The thought of staying here any longer filled him with a sinking dread. 'No,' he stated firmly. 'I want to go home. Now.'

'I don't think that's advisable—' the doctor began, a concerned frown pinching her brow.

'I feel fine. I don't want to take up a bed unnecessarily when someone who's really sick could use it. I'll be okay at home,' Caleb said gruffly. He wasn't used to people telling him what he could and couldn't do and it rankled.

'I really don't think—'

'I don't care what you think. I'm going home,' he said, levering himself up and readying himself to swing his legs out of bed.

The only way he was staying here was if they called Security and tied him down.

The doctor sighed as if she'd seen this scenario before and knew there was no way to stop someone like this once they'd made up their mind.

'I can't prevent you from leaving, Señor Araya, but I must insist you don't go home on your own,' she said sternly. 'You'll need someone responsible there to keep an eye on you in case there are any after-effects from the head injury. The CAT scan we gave you didn't show up anything worrying, but it's better to be safe.'

Frustration rattled through him. He just wanted to be at home now, without people fussing over him any more.

'I'll be fine. I can call my GP if I start to feel ill,' he bit out.

The doctor shook her head. 'That's not good enough. You need someone there with you full-time for the next forty-eight hours at least.'

Elena must have sensed his unease because she stepped forwards and said, 'I can stay with him, at his home.'

The doctor studied her for a moment. 'Are you his partner?'

There was an infinitesimal pause before Elena said, 'Yes.'

He glanced at her in surprise but she didn't turn to catch his eye, just kept her steady, confident gaze trained on the doctor.

The doctor nodded, seeming to decide that Elena was a sensible and trustworthy sort of person.

He could see why. She certainly gave that impression. Caleb really liked that about her. She was no-nonsense, just the kind of person he liked to have around. He couldn't do with women who simpered and flapped about ineffectually. Having her at home with him for a short while would be fine by him. It might even give him more time to try and figure out the real state of their relationship. He was positive there had to be more to it than 'just friends', as she'd claimed.

Turning back to Caleb now and fixing him with a steely stare, the doctor asked, 'Have you been sick since you woke up or had any dizziness? Any memory loss?'

Out of the corner of his eye he saw Elena

stiffen and waited for her to tell the doctor about his elusive memory, preparing himself for a fight, but when he turned to look directly at her she just gazed back at him with those bright, intelligent eyes of hers, her mouth firmly shut. A strange kind of unspoken agreement seemed to pass between them and he realised she was letting him know that she was on his side.

She wasn't going to give him up.

Well, that proved something at least; she must care about him if she was willing to twist the truth to help him get out of here. The thought warmed him.

'No, I feel fine,' he said, tearing his gaze away from her to look at the doctor again, feeling the weight of anxiety begin to lift from his chest.

The doctor nodded, apparently convinced that he was telling the truth. 'Okay then, I'll go and fill out the paperwork. You'll need to come in next week for further tests though, Señor Araya, to make sure we haven't missed anything.'

Caleb nodded but didn't say anything. He'd deal with all that later. He just wanted to get out of here now.

'I'll let you get dressed then. Your clothes and personal effects will be in the cupboard at the side of your bed,' the doctor said, moving towards the door. 'You might need a bit of help getting dressed because of the pain in your rib. I can call a nurse if you like,' she said, turning back with an expectant look on her face.

'I don't need a nurse,' he said dismissively.

'I can help him if he needs me to,' Elena chimed in, throwing him a chiding look.

The doctor just nodded briskly.

'Thank you, Doctor,' Elena added, giving the woman a warm smile.

Once the doctor had left the room, Elena busied herself by pulling all his things out of the bedside cabinet and laying them out on the bed. Picking up his shirt, she looked at it with her nose wrinkled. 'I'm afraid there's some blood on this from where you cut your head.'

'I don't care about that. Pass it to me, will you,' he said, reaching out for the clothing and wincing as his cracked rib made itself known.

She batted his hand away, frowning. 'I'll do it. If you can just sit up a bit more—'

Ignoring his huff of frustration, she put one hand carefully behind each shoulder and pulled gently, forcing him to sit up enough so she could slip the shirt around his back and hold it out for him to slide his arms into the sleeves.

Her hands had been cool and the sensation of her skin on his hot flesh lingered there while she leant in to do the buttons up for him.

Her nearness made him want to pull her in for another kiss but, despite his still rather woolly-headed state, he was aware that it would be a highly inappropriate thing to do.

He growled with irritation, hating how weak and vulnerable he must appear to her right now. 'This is ridiculous. I'm not a child. I can do my own buttons up!'

A small smile lifted the corners of her mouth and she raised an eyebrow at him. 'Stop being so proud and let me help. If you won't let me take care of you I'm going to have to tell the doctor that I can't go home with you after all and you'll have to stay in the hospital with the nurses fussing around you instead.'

He let out a harrumphing noise, but let her do the rest of the buttons up. Despite feeling annoyed that she was using his injuries against him, he was impressed that she hadn't been upset by his shortness and obviously wasn't about to let it put her off coming home with him.

Most women would have let him have his way and backed off, but it seemed that Elena wasn't most women.

He drew the line though when she tried to help him get out of bed and firmly batted her outstretched hand away as he swung his legs out. He pulled on his suit trousers over the boxers he was mercifully still wearing, managing after a moment or two of pained fumbling to pull the zip up and hook the fastener, then sat for a moment to catch his breath.

'Is this your address?' Elena asked as he slowly levered himself up off the bed, fighting back a wave of nausea as he stood up and felt a heavy weight of darkness pressing down on his head.

He must have moved too quickly.

Blinking hard to clear his vision, he stared at the driving licence she was holding up, which was sandwiched behind a clear plastic window in his wallet.

'That's it,' he said, taking a long breath to steady himself.

'Okay, I'll go and arrange for a taxi to take us home,' she said, giving him a pointed glance that said, *Take it easy until I get back.*

He got the distinct feeling that this was only the beginning of his time being ordered around by this woman.

To his surprise, he found he didn't entirely hate the idea.

The cab drew up in front of the building where Caleb lived and Elena swallowed hard, her stomach doing a slow somersault now they'd reached their destination.

It had been fine in the hospital while she was distracted by the practical aspects of getting Caleb home, but now they were finally here, and were going to be totally alone for the first time since the disastrous meeting this morning—where she'd had a worrying amount of trouble keeping her emotions under wraps—she was beginning to regret her rash promise to look after him for the next couple of days.

She was determined to follow it through though—because she owed him. If it hadn't been for her he never would have had the accident in the first place.

The moment she'd sensed how determined he was to get out of hospital she'd made a snap decision. Not calling out his lie to the doctor about his memory being sound had almost been a step too far for her, but she'd told herself that if she stuck with him around the clock she'd be able to alert the doctors the moment he seemed to be even vaguely struggling. In the busy hospital he could have been left alone for long periods of time, but here in his house she'd be there to keep an eye on him every second of the day.

Unless he suddenly remembered that he hated her and sent her away, of course.

Her stomach did another sickening flip.

If that happened he'd be left alone in his apartment without anyone there to look out for him. And what if he passed out or fell and hurt himself once she'd gone?

She took a steadying breath then blew it out towards the sky, imagining it was her fears she was expelling as they exploded into a million pieces in her mind.

No. She wasn't going to worry about that right now. Hopefully, if he did remember what had happened between them, the fact that she'd helped bail him out of hospital and offered to stick around to take care of him would at least make him pause before chucking her out. If she was really lucky, her presence here might even prove to him that she was genuinely sorry for what had happened in the past and that she was serious about wanting to make amends for hurting him.

That she still cared about him.

Not that she'd ever really stopped, even when she'd pushed him away.

'Elena?' Caleb said beside her and she could tell from the tone of his voice that he was wondering what the heck she was doing, still sitting here like a lemon when they'd reached their destination.

'Are you sure you want to come in with me?' he asked brusquely. 'You don't have to, you know. I can take care of myself from here.'

She turned to fix him with a stern glare. 'No, you can't, Caleb; you heard what the doctor said. You need someone around, especially if you're still feeling a bit confused.'

He shrugged as if it was neither here nor there to him whether she stayed or not, but she could have sworn she saw a flash of a smile in his eyes.

'Okay, let's go,' she said, opening the cab door and telling herself that the best thing all round was just to take one step at a time and deal with any consequences as and when they came.

Caleb's penthouse apartment was breathtaking, and exactly the sort of place she would have expected him to choose to live. Light poured in through the large warehouse-style windows, bathing the stylish but comfortable-looking furniture in soft spring sunlight. The colours he'd chosen to furnish the place were earthy and muted in a warm and comforting way, with terracotta tiles on the floor and dark tan leather and stained wood sofas and tables gathered in the middle of the vast space. It was a really restful room to be in and Elena let out a breath as she felt herself relax a little.

She was still acutely aware that she was here under false pretences, but she reassured herself that this was about making sure Caleb was safe and cared for; it had nothing whatsoever to do with her trying to persuade him to listen to her business proposal. She'd deal with all that once he was fully well again. There was no way she'd take advantage of his lapse in memory.

She was here as his friend, nothing more.

His only friend, by the sounds of it.

Judging by the fact he didn't have anyone obvious to call upon when he was in the hospital, she guessed she wasn't the only one he'd kept at arm's length.

The thought of how alone he was made sorrow well heavily in her gut.

She knew she should have sought him out before now. She'd wanted to, had for years, but she'd never quite plucked up the courage to face him again—until it had been absolutely essential. That made her a coward, she knew that, but she'd always been afraid of how out of control Caleb made her feel and she'd needed every ounce of strength over the intervening years to build a successful career for herself. It wasn't easy being a woman in a male-dominated arena.

At least that was what she was telling herself.

The passion of his kiss earlier came back to haunt her as he walked past her into the living area and she caught the unique scent of him in the air.

Moving quickly away from him, she marched into the kitchen diner at the other end of the large room, aware that her heart was racing, and pretended to be admiring the high-tech gadgets he had in there to give herself a moment to pull herself together.

'Can I make you something to eat? Or drink?' she asked, turning back to look at him. He was standing by the largest sofa, watching her with a perplexed sort of frown.

'You don't need to mollycoddle me, Elena—I can fix my own food. In fact, I should be cooking for you to say thanks for bailing me out at the hospital.'

She held up a hand. 'Not a chance. Unless your cooking skills have improved since university?' she said with a slow grin.

He threw her a look of mock offence. 'Was it that bad?' He frowned. 'I don't re-member.'

'It was passable,' she said, her mouth still twitching with mirth at the memory of it.

In truth, it had been terrible. The one time he'd cooked for her, when she'd gone over to his place to study for an exam, she'd pulled such a face after the first mouthful that Caleb had scraped the lot into the bin and called for takeout pizza instead.

'Well, like I said earlier, you don't have to stay here with me; I'll be fine,' he said, sitting down carefully on the sofa and winc-ing a little as his rib appeared to give him trouble.

She folded her arms. 'Like *I* said, there's no way I'm leaving you alone.'

She'd always stood up to him like this, refusing to be intimidated by his gruff de-meanour, but deep down his dominating personality had twisted her into knots, threatening her carefully constructed cool.

Fifteen years ago he'd made her question everything she'd thought she wanted in a man. He was bold and charismatic, but he also seemed exactly the sort to smash her heart to pieces should things go wrong between them. At the time she wasn't prepared to put herself in danger of that happening, not after working so hard to get into her first choice of university and make her first move towards the kind of life she'd always dreamed of building for herself.

But she hadn't been able to stay away from him.

Struggling to keep her feelings under control, she'd found the safest thing had been to pretend that they didn't exist. It had been the only way to protect herself.

Except that somewhere along the line that had stopped working.

Caleb could sense that Elena wasn't altogether comfortable being here in his apartment with him and he wondered again what it was she wasn't telling him.

'If you're worried about where you're going to sleep, you're welcome to take one of the guest rooms.' He pointed towards a door that led to the corridor of four bedrooms.

'Okay, thank you,' she said a little distractedly.

'Is there somewhere else you need to be today?' he asked, concerned now that he was keeping her from something important. The last thing he wanted was to be a burden to her.

'No, nowhere,' she answered, coming to sit down on an armchair opposite where he sat, finally giving him her full attention.

A sense of relief took him by surprise. He was still feeling pretty woozy and disorientated and it was soothing to know she'd be staying there with him for a while. Even if she did feel like a total stranger to him at the moment.

'So, *friend*, I guess I need to get to know you all over again. Do you have a partner? Husband? Boyfriend in England?' he asked.

She recoiled a little, as if the question had caught her by surprise. 'Not at the moment. I've been too busy recently with work to hold down a serious relationship.'

'When you say recently—?'

She flashed him a self-conscious smile. 'For the last few years.'

'You haven't had a serious relationship for a *few years*?'

She shrugged as she smoothed her hands

down the sides of her skirt. 'I've dated, but I've not clicked with anyone.'

'I find that hard to believe.'

The air between them seemed to throb with tension and she gave him a strained smile, then glanced away.

He was making her uncomfortable. But why?

'Elena?'

She looked back at him, her expression now impassive, as if she'd pulled a mask back into place. 'Do you mind if I make myself a drink?' she said suddenly, slapping her hands onto her knees. 'I'm dying for a cup of tea.'

He frowned at the sudden change of subject but didn't press her on the reason for it. Perhaps she was just tired after the stress and strain of the day. He was pretty tired himself now, even though he'd slept for a lot of it. 'Sure, help yourself,' he said.

She got up and walked over to the kitchen. 'Would you like one?' she asked, reaching for the kettle on the work surface.

'No, thanks.' He sat forward in his seat. 'I should take a shower.' He sniffed at his shirt, inhaling the institutional smell of stringent cleaning fluid and decay and, just like that, a memory flew to the front of his mind and he knew why he'd wanted to get out of that hospital so quickly.

His anguish must have shown on his face because Elena said, 'Caleb? Is everything okay? Did you remember something?' her voice sounding breathy with concern.

'Just why I wanted to leave the hospital. My mother died about six months ago and I spent an awful lot of time visiting her in one.'

The expression on her face changed from worry to one of sympathy. 'Your PA told me. I'm so sorry for your loss,' she said, her bright blue eyes soft with compassion.

He nodded, accepting her condolences, and ran a hand over his face, feeling stubble rasp at his palm.

There was something more to the memory of losing his mother but he couldn't put his finger on what it was. Some kind of underlying emotion bubbling under the surface, not quite clear enough for him to fully grasp.

'I don't seem to be able to remember a lot about her at the moment. I know the time I spent with her at the end of her life was… difficult…but I'm not entirely sure why.'

Elena folded her arms and leant against the counter top. 'From what you've told me about her, I don't think you were particularly close, at least not when you were younger. You were keen to move away from the place where you grew up and she didn't want you to.'

She looked at him, as if expecting this to jog his memory, but nothing new came to him.

Sadness swelled in his chest.

What was wrong with him? Why was he getting maudlin all of a sudden? Perhaps the trauma to his head was somehow affecting his emotional state. That had to be it. He knew it wasn't his usual way to discuss how he was feeling with anyone, particularly not a woman. It was one of the things that had contributed to destroying his relationship with his ex-fiancée. Her constant need to try and get into his head and fix him had caused him to feel both hounded and suffocated.

There was something about Elena that invited confidences though.

But what was it?

A half-formed answer flitted around the edges of his mind, just out of reach, and he pushed an unnerving resurgence of panic away, telling himself there was no point in trying to force his memory to come back; it would reappear in its own good time. Perhaps after he'd had a good night's sleep in his own bed.

He stood up carefully, relieved to find his dizziness had subsided, and started to make his way towards the door to the corridor that led through to his bedroom and en suite bathroom.

'Where are you going?' Elena asked, dashing out of the kitchen to intercept him.

He bristled at her bossy tone. 'I told you, I need a shower.'

'Not on your own. What if you get dizzy and fall?'

'Are you offering to join me?' he asked with a teasing smile, feeling his pulse pick up at the thought of it.

She visibly tensed, then shot him a cool, reproving smile. 'I'll wait in your bedroom, just in case you need me,' she said, turning on the spot and striding away from him, her body language looking a little stiff and awkward now.

He wanted to call after her that he wouldn't need her, that he didn't need anybody, that he was fine on his own. But he had the oddest feeling that that wasn't the case at all.

CHAPTER FOUR

CALEB MANAGED FINE by himself in the shower, despite the sharp pain that shot through his chest every time he moved his left arm. Checking over his body now that he was naked, he was shocked to see how much of it was covered in angry-looking bruises. It made him realise just how lightly he'd got off considering he'd been hit by a motorbike.

Or so he'd been told.

He still couldn't remember a thing about it.

Tamping down on the now familiar swell of unease, he wrapped a towel tightly around his waist and stared at himself in the mirror, tentatively touching the raised bump in his hairline where he'd hit his head. Perhaps all his errant memories were trapped in the bump and when it went down they'd be released back into his brain.

He shook his head at himself, wondering where his normally sane self had disappeared to. He really didn't feel like himself at the moment. There was a strange sense of having lost something heavy from deep within him, as if a weight he'd been carrying around had lifted from his body and was hovering somewhere over his head.

Or perhaps the accident had just knocked all the sense out of him.

Whatever it was, the best thing he could do right now was carry on as normal. There was no way he was letting a slight blip in memory and a small fracture stop him from functioning properly.

Giving his reflection a firm nod, he turned away from the mirror and left the en suite.

He expected to find Elena waiting there for him and was preparing to bat away any help she tried to offer and prove to her he wasn't as frail and vulnerable as she clearly suspected he was, so was surprised—and, if he was honest, a little disappointed—to find the room empty.

The sound of voices floated in through the open bedroom door and he heard the swish and click of the front door closing, then the gentle pad of feet on the hallway tiles as someone walked towards the bedroom.

'Oh, you're out,' Elena said as she emerged in the doorway, her cheeks flushing with colour as she eyed him standing there with just a towel slung around his hips.

He suppressed a smile as she averted her gaze and pretended to be studying a picture on the wall next to her, as if making a point of not staring at his half-naked body.

'Who was at the door?' he asked.

'Benita.'

'What did she want?'

'She brought your mobile phone over, which you'd left on your desk. She thought you'd want it, but I told her you wouldn't be dealing with anything work-related today because you need to rest.' She turned to look at him now, her expression serious. 'I also said that you wouldn't be back in the office for a while.'

'You did, huh? Well, unfortunately, I don't have time to be off work right now.' He held out his hand. 'I'll take the phone.'

When she flashed him an I-don't-think-so expression he added a determined, 'Thank you.'

'Caleb, I really don't think you should—'

'I'm not interested in what you think,' he said, feeling irritation prick at the back of his neck.

But, instead of handing the phone over like most people would have done when he used that tone of voice, she crossed her arms and fixed him with a hard stare.

'There is no way I'm giving you this phone tonight. You need to rest and get a good night's sleep and you're not going to do that if you're worrying about what's going on at work without you. I'm sure you've hired an exceptional team of staff and they're more than capable of handling things there without you for a couple of days.'

He glared at her in disbelief. No one ever talked to him like that and it was rather shocking to have her facing off with him, especially here in his own home. In his own bedroom.

'How do you intend to stop me from taking it from you?' he asked, putting on an amused smile to cover his incredulity.

She didn't even blink. 'By doing this,' she said, lifting open the front of her blouse and sliding the phone down inside the neck, so that it nestled in between her breasts.

He swallowed hard. There was no way he could physically try to take it from her now. Even though he ached to. Very much.

'Cute,' he growled, his frustration coming over loud and clear.

She smiled serenely. 'Someone has to save you from yourself.'

'I don't need saving,' he ground out, folding his arms.

'I beg to differ. I know you, Caleb; you'll work all night tonight to make up for the time you lost in the hospital.'

He frowned. 'How would you know that?'

'Because you regularly worked through the night when we were at university to make up for any time you lost.'

'That sounds like me,' he said slowly, as the unsettling feeling of not remembering his university days bit at his nerves again.

'So I'm staging an intervention. Again.'

'Again? What else have you kept so close

to your chest from me?' he asked, raising a suggestive eyebrow.

Her jaw appeared to tighten and she frowned. 'I mean it's not the only time I've had to point out that you work too hard, that's all,' she said, looking a little uncomfortable now.

Despite the fact he could probably have held both of her wrists in one hand and easily retrieved his phone, he could tell from the steely look in her eyes that she wouldn't tolerate such behaviour.

Frustration pinched at him. He was going to have to let her win this one.

'Right, well, now that's settled I'll leave you to get dressed,' Elena said, her mouth twitching at the corner with what looked like suppressed amusement.

She was enjoying ordering him around. Damn her.

As soon as she'd walked away he strode to the door and swung it shut with a little more force than was entirely necessary.

Okay, so he was grateful to her for helping him get out of the hospital, but he had the unsettling feeling he would have been better off staying there if this was the kind of treatment he was going to have to put up with for the next couple of days.

Elena walked out of the room with blood rushing loudly in her ears. She couldn't quite believe she'd just hidden his phone down her top, but it had been obvious he wasn't going to allow himself to rest if she didn't force him to. After an accident like this he needed time to recover and heal. Especially as it appeared his memory still hadn't fully returned—even though he was clearly trying to brush that tiny detail under the carpet.

She was painfully aware that she'd know the moment it all came back to him because she'd probably find herself out on her ear.

Though hopefully that wouldn't happen any time soon.

The phone pressed uncomfortably against her breastbone as she walked away from him and as soon as she reached one of the spare bedrooms she removed it and stuffed it under the mattress at the side of the bed she always slept on. If he came into the room to look for it while she was asleep— just the thought of *that* gave her the jitters—

he'd have to lift both her and the mattress up in order to get to it.

Not that she believed for a second he'd actually do that. He was too proud. She had wondered for one panicked moment earlier though whether he'd ignore her insistence that he took the evening off work and stuff his hand down her blouse to grab his phone, but luckily decorum had prevailed. She gave a little shiver. That would have been altogether too much to handle. She'd already been struggling to hold it together in his half-dressed, badly bruised presence, and his touching her like that would have tipped her right over the edge. Into what, she wasn't quite sure. But it was definitely better not to find out.

Flopping back onto the bed, she ran her hand over her eyes, which felt gritty and sore with tiredness. She was exhausted now after all the stress of the day, not to mention the tension she was carrying around with her, worrying about her staff and the fate of her business.

There was a loud rap at the door and she sat up quickly, smoothing her hair away from her face, not wanting Caleb to see any kind of chink in her armour.

He strode into the room, thankfully dressed now in a pair of faded jeans and a casual shirt, which fitted him so well she suspected they must have cost a fortune, despite their lived-in appearance.

'Will you be okay sleeping in here?' he asked, his eyes scanning the room as if checking for anything that might be wrong with it.

'Yes, thanks, I'll be fine.'

'Okay, well, if you're not going to give me my phone back I'm going to watch TV in the living room for a few minutes, then go to bed. You're welcome to join me—' he shot her a wicked grin '—watching television, I mean.'

'Er…no, thank you. I have a bit of work to catch up on, so I'll stay in here so I don't disturb you,' she said, giving him a strained smile back and trying to ignore the warmth blooming between her thighs at the mere suggestion of sharing his bed. The most disconcerting thing was that she wasn't entirely sure whether he was genuinely flirting with her, or just teasing her to get his own back for her phone-hiding stunt.

She guessed the latter, knowing from experience how much he struggled with not being fully in control of every situation.

'How's your head now?' she asked, keeping her hands folded in her lap so he wouldn't see how nervous she was having him loom over her while she sat on the bed.

'It's fine. I have a low-level headache but pieces of my memory seem to be coming back now.' He looked away from her as a strained expression flitted over his face, proving to her that she'd been right about him trying to hide how unsettled he really felt about it.

She wanted to reach out to him, to somehow soothe away his worry with her touch, but she was acutely aware that it would be entirely inappropriate considering their former relationship.

'I'm sure it'll all come back soon, perhaps after a good rest.'

He nodded, his expression now coolly nonchalant. 'I hope you'll be comfortable in here,' he said brusquely. 'There are some

T-shirts in there if you want something to sleep in,' he added, waving towards a wardrobe on the other side of the room.

'Thank you,' she said, touched that he was concerned about her comfort. 'Is there anything I can do for you?' she blurted as he began to turn away from her.

His slow, loaded grin made her insides swoop but she ignored the feeling, continuing to look at him steadily until he shook his head.

'Nothing, Elena. I'm fine. I'll see you in the morning.' And, with that, he turned on the spot and exited the room, leaving his tantalising, clean scent hanging in the air behind him.

Flopping back onto the bed again, she took a deep calming breath, willing her heartbeat to slow down. It was so unnerving, being here in Caleb's house as a guest. She almost didn't want to go to sleep in case she woke up to find him back to the beast of a man she'd encountered this morning in his meeting room.

She'd enjoyed seeing the small flashes of his personality coming through since they'd left the hospital though and part of her ached to join him in the living room and push him to show her some more of them.

But she knew, deep down, that that could be a dangerous game to play.

No, she'd leave her door open to keep an ear out for him in case he needed her, but it was probably best to give him a bit of space now.

After getting washed in the en suite in her room and changing into one of the large, soft cotton T-shirts Caleb had loaned her she slid beneath the sheets and lay listening to the low murmur of the television in the other room, feeling exhaustion dragging at her eyelids until she could no longer keep them open.

She slept fitfully, her dreams punctuated with disturbing images from the accident.

Waking up in the early hours with her heart racing, she had a sudden panic that Caleb might have had a turn for the worse in his sleep and she slipped out of bed to tiptoe silently to his room to check on him. Pushing the door open quietly, she was confused to find his bed empty and looking as though it hadn't been slept in all night.

Where was he? Had he left the apartment without her knowing?

Blood pulsed hard in her head as she moved quickly down the corridor, checking the other rooms, which all appeared to be empty, then ran into the living area, her heartbeat erratic now.

Relief rushed through her as she spotted him lying on the sofa nearest the windows with a laptop perched precariously on his lap, breathing gently, his face smoothed of its usual fierceness in repose.

She stood and watched him sleeping for a while, letting the still and silent darkness envelop her as she tried to get a handle on the intense rush of feelings that cascaded through her.

She'd cared so deeply for him once, had thought at one point that her future would be with him by her side, but then she'd blown it, naïvely choosing the safe—boring, as Caleb had called it—option instead.

Looking at him now, she realised with a surge of emotion that she missed him. So intensely it hurt. Over the intervening years she'd been able to quash the waves of regret she'd experienced in her weaker moments, but she knew now that she still craved the elated, excited way he'd made her feel, like a habit she couldn't kick.

She wasn't here to get him back though, she told herself sternly, forcing herself to unclench her fists as she walked quietly over to where he lay to lift the laptop off his lap so she could take it back to the bedroom with her—just in case he woke up and decided to keep working. It was highly unlikely he'd ever trust her again, not after the way she'd let him down.

He was altogether too proud for that.

But she was determined to make it up to him somehow. Perhaps, if she was lucky, once he was better he'd remember this time they'd spent together and decide it was worth giving their friendship another chance.

Tiptoeing out of the room, she glanced back briefly to where he lay sleeping, his chest rising and falling in a steady rhythm.

All she could do now was hope for the best.

Caleb woke bleary-eyed from such a heavy sleep it took him a few moments to figure out where he was.

As the room came into focus he realised he was lying on the sofa in his living room.

Huh, strange.

Levering himself up to a sitting position, he felt a twinge of pain in his chest and the memory of waking up in the hospital yesterday after an accident came flooding back. As did the baffling appearance of the beautiful woman who had turned up to take care of him. A woman he couldn't remember ever seeing before in his life.

Though he knew her. He *knew* her.

And why did he feel as though there was something more to their friendship?

Feeling his heart rate begin to rise, he forced the perturbing question out of his head for now and turned his attention to what he usually thought about upon waking instead.

His business.

He hadn't intended to work for long last night—just wanting to make sure he hadn't missed anything important whilst he'd been at the hospital—and had brought out the laptop he'd had stashed under the coffee table, feeling a sense of relief that Elena hadn't noticed and confiscated that too. After skimming a number of things that didn't require his urgent attention, the words beginning to blur together in front of his tired eyes, he'd come across a message from Benita that had made him start with worry, causing him to wince with pain as his cracked rib complained.

He'd turned the problem over and over in his mind for a while, desperately trying to keep his attention focused on solving this hiccup, but his tired brain had had other ideas, insistently pulling him into a deep, overpowering sleep.

He was awake now though.

Reaching down onto his lap where he'd left his laptop, he was confused to find it wasn't there. He sat up carefully, mindful of his damaged rib, and felt along the floor next to the sofa, guessing it must have slipped off his knee whilst he was asleep.

'Looking for this?' came a softly chastising voice from the other side of the room and he turned his head to see a woman—Elena—standing there with his computer held between her hands. Her brow was creased and her expression guarded.

'I thought you were going to give your

poor brain a rest last night so it had a chance to recover.'

He shrugged and swung his legs off the sofa, then stood up carefully, turning to face her. Twisting his body was not at all comfortable at the moment.

'Like I said, I don't have time to take a break right now.'

She huffed out a sigh. 'Why not?'

He threw up his hands in frustration, wincing at the twinge of pain this caused. 'Because there are things going on that need my immediate attention.'

'Like what?'

Clearly she wasn't going to give up her questioning. He wasn't entirely sure he could trust her with details about his business, but something in him, something he couldn't identify, told him it would be okay to talk to her.

He sighed. 'I need to convince a potential American supplier of my small appliance-sized battery that I'm an easy and reliable person to partner with,' he muttered, folding his arms and rocking back on his heels as he thought about the problem again.

'Apparently he has concerns and is considering backing out of a meeting I've taken great pains to set up while he's over here in Spain. He's supposed to be coming to Araya Industries on the last day of his visit and I'd hoped to persuade him to include one of my rechargeable batteries in their product range.'

Walking over to the kitchen, he opened the fridge and extracted a carton of orange juice, which he held up towards her to ask if she'd like some. When she nodded, he grabbed two glasses and poured them both a good measure of it.

'According to Benita, his PA let slip he'd heard a rumour about me being a difficult man to work with and is considering taking a meeting with one of my competitors instead—who is apparently the stable, patriarchal type that Carter prefers to work with.' He put the carton back into the fridge and slammed the door shut, noticing her jump a little at the forcefulness with which he did this.

Taking a calming breath, he picked up one of the glasses and handed it to her, then grabbed his own and took a long drink from it.

He really needed to keep his cool here if he was going to get on top of this problem. Especially as he was still having a bit of trouble thinking straight after the accident.

'The fact that I don't have a partner, let alone a wife, is troubling to him,' he said, running a hand over his face, trying to wake himself up a bit. 'But if I can convince him I'm a good bet it could be a hugely lucrative deal that would give us a strong foothold in the American market.'

'How are you going to do that? Convince him, I mean,' Elena asked, looking at him from over the rim of her glass.

'I'm going to offer to take him and his wife out for dinner tonight and show them I'm not the ogre they seem to think I am,' he said decisively.

'You're going to meet them on your own?'

He hesitated, thinking about this. 'It's better if I don't make it too business-formal, so I don't think I should take anyone else from the office,' he said slowly. 'It needs to be a more laid-back affair.'

'But you're concerned it might confirm his suspicions about you if you turn up on your own.'

His gaze snapped to hers. How did she seem to know what he was thinking? It was as if she could read his addled mind.

She shrugged a shoulder. 'I know you don't remember, but I run my own manufacturing engineering company in England and I've been in a similar situation before. In my experience it's better to have someone else to make up a four, especially if he's bringing his wife.'

He ran a hand across his jaw, frustration needling him. 'I don't have a girlfriend at the moment and I haven't worked with Benita long enough to build up a convincing rapport with her.'

'No,' Elena said, making it sound as if taking Benita would be the last thing she'd suggest.

'And it would be helpful to have someone who knows something about the industry and how to behave in business meetings already,' he said as an idea began to form in his head.

'That's true, especially as your memory isn't exactly at its best right now.'

'So that only leaves one person,' he said,

folding his arms and giving her a pointed stare.

'Who?' she asked, frowning at first, then widening her eyes as she caught on to just what he was suggesting.

'That's right, Elena. *You.*'

CHAPTER FIVE

'ME?' ELENA'S HEART leapt into her throat.

Caleb gave her a firm smile, as if the matter had already been decided.

Though, to be fair, she guessed it had.

There was no way she could refuse to help him, of course. For one thing, she couldn't let him go out on his own when his head injury was still an issue, and for another she was keenly aware that this could be the perfect opportunity to atone for the way she'd treated him in their younger years. She could really help him here—do something of substance.

'It's the ideal solution,' he said, nodding sagely.

'How are we going to convince them we're a couple when you don't remember a thing about me though?' she asked, her nerves biting a little.

He waved a hand, dismissing her concern. 'We'll do a cramming session before the meeting.'

She swallowed, feeling tension building in her throat. She was going to have to be careful what she told him if she was going to avoid the small matter of her being his number one enemy.

'Okay, well, I'll need to dash over to the hotel where I'm staying first and fetch my bag so I can change. I'll need something more appropriate to wear to dinner,' she said, gesturing to her now rather crumpled suit.

And she could do with a few minutes on her own to get her head together.

'Which hotel are you staying in?' he asked.

'The Barcelona Gran Mar, near the beach.'

He looked at her long and hard for a moment. 'Okay, I'll come with you. We can walk from here; it's not far.'

Her stomach sank. 'No, you should stay here and rest.'

'I'm fine,' he said in that no-nonsense manner she knew so well. 'Anyway, how are you going to keep your beady eye on me otherwise?'

She sighed and shook her head at his droll expression. The man had an answer for everything. It had been the same when they were younger too.

'Okay, fine, come with me then. Perhaps you can point out some of the famous landmarks on the way. I've not had a chance to see any of them since I arrived.'

She waited while Caleb put in a call to Benita, asking her to get hold of Carter's PA and arrange a dinner meeting for that evening. Once he'd hung up, they shrugged on their jackets and left the apartment, Elena's heart beating at twice its usual speed as she contemplated the idea of spending the whole day with Caleb by her side.

Gaudi's mesmerising art nouveau Casa Milà building was only a couple of streets away from Caleb's apartment, fortuitously in the right direction for her hotel near the Nova Icaria beach, so they strolled past it, Elena admiring the strange, cave-like curves and outlandish quirks of the architecture. The whole building looked as though it had been hand-carved out of an enormous piece of rock by prehistoric man, looking truly anachronistic next to its more modern neighbours.

'He really was a genius,' she said in wonder, gazing up at the breathtaking façade. 'Such a visionary.'

'Unparalleled,' Caleb agreed, using his hand to shield his eyes against the bright glare of the sun as he squinted up at it. 'You know, I'm a little embarrassed to admit this, but I barely notice it's there any more. It's become part of the street furniture to me after all my years living here.'

'That's terrible,' Elena said, frowning up at the building.

'I'm so busy getting from one place to another I forget to look up,' he murmured.

She glanced at him. 'I do the same thing in London,' she said, feeling a little rush of poignancy that their lives had followed such a parallel path, despite the distance between them. 'It's very easy to take beauty for granted,' she added.

'Yes.' He paused then said, 'It's funny, but losing big chunks of my past seems to have brought the present into sharper focus.'

When she looked round at him she experienced a little frisson at the intense way he was looking at her.

'Are you happy with your life?' she blurted, her nerves getting the better of her.

His brow furrowed as he thought about this. 'I'm satisfied with the way my business is growing and I enjoy living in Barcelona.'

There was a heavy pause while she waited for him to continue. 'And, for the purposes of our dinner this evening, I'm very happy with my love life.' He flashed her a wolfish grin, making her tummy flip over.

He gestured for them to start walking again and she fell into step with him as they made their way along the pavement, feeling even more jumpy now than when they'd first started out.

'Speaking of which, I guess we ought to decide how long we've been an item, for the purpose of tonight's charade,' Caleb said, a wry grin turning up the corner of his mouth.

Elena took a breath, feeling her pulse jitter. 'Yes, I guess we should get our story straight. How about we tell them that we met at university but were just friends then, and bumped into each other again a year ago at a business conference and things progressed from there.'

'Dull, but believable, I suppose,' Caleb said with a thoughtful nod.

A coach had parked a little way down the street and as they approached it the pavement suddenly became overrun by a large tour group that filed off to look at the famous building they'd just left.

She felt Caleb slip his arm protectively around her as they began to be jostled by the crowd moving past them and she allowed herself to sink against his strong body for a moment, her heart beginning to race as she breathed in his zesty, familiar scent.

Once they were clear of the crowd he let her go and she dazedly rubbed at her arm where his hand had gripped her, her skin feeling tingly and sensitive where their bodies had connected.

'You're going to have to get used to me touching you,' Caleb said in a low voice, looking at her arm where she was rubbing it. 'Or they're not going to believe we're a couple.'

Elena swallowed hard, balling her fists.

'Yes, of course. You just took me by surprise then, that's all.'

He looked at her with one eyebrow raised. 'Were you always this jumpy around me?'

'No, no! I'm just a little off balance today. This is all a bit strange, to be honest.' She flashed him a strained smile. 'You have to admit, we've got ourselves into a rather odd situation here.'

She tried not to notice the puzzled look he gave her and strode on confidently, looking deliberately around her, at anything but him, to give her some time to pull herself together.

Good grief, if she couldn't even act normally around him when they were on their own how was she going to manage it when they had an audience tonight?

She needed to get herself into a more relaxed and *friendly* mindset.

A little further on they walked past Gaudi's Sagrada Família, which rose majestically into the sky like a discarded giant elf king's crown.

'It makes me think of something from the *Lord of the Rings*,' Elena said in wonder as she took in the arresting quirkiness of it.

'We spent a whole weekend at university once, working our way through the trilogy of films. I could barely keep my eyes open at the end of it and I dreamt about it intensively for the next few nights.' She glanced at him speculatively. 'Do you remember?'

He shook his head, agitation flashing in his eyes. 'I have no recollection of ever seeing those films.'

Her heart went out to him. It must be so distressing for him to lose so many of his memories—though, now she thought about it, the hard shell she'd witnessed at their initial meeting had definitely softened a little since they'd been gone. Perhaps the absence of deep-seated anger that had driven him for most of his life was finally allowing his true nature to emerge from the dark place where it had been hiding.

'Well, perhaps you should think of it as a good thing,' she said with forced jollity, in an attempt to lighten the sombre atmosphere that seemed to have fallen between them now. 'You get to experience the excitement of watching them afresh. I wish I could do that.'

His eyebrow shot up. 'Losing the first

twenty-five years of your life is a high price to pay though, don't you think?'

She shrugged. 'I think it's worth taking every positive you can out of an experience. Even if it is a testing one.'

'You're quite the optimist,' Caleb drawled, raising a derisive eyebrow.

Her skin prickled with annoyance. 'And you're a cynic! Life's too short to dwell on the negative.'

Although perhaps she should learn to take her own advice, she thought wryly, considering how much anxiety she seemed to be carrying around with her at the moment.

Caleb looked taken aback at her outburst, but after a moment his features softened and he let out a low laugh. 'Maybe you're right,' he said. 'I have little enough "life" outside of the business as it is; I guess I should spend it enjoying what I work so hard to have.'

They walked on again in silence for a minute, their arms swinging at their sides.

'To be fair, I'm just as bad about spending too much time working and not enjoying all life has to offer,' Elena said after a while. 'I can regularly spend up to ten hours a day at work and sometimes carry on into the evenings if I need to. I've lost count of the number of parties and get-togethers I've cried off recently. My friends despair of me.'

'You don't go out much?' he asked.

'Not as much as I should. There's no wonder I'm single; my personal life could definitely do with some TLC.'

'Why have you *really* been on your own for so long?' he asked in such a casual tone she felt sure he'd been waiting for the right opportunity to broach that question.

So this was it then—time to be totally honest with him.

'Well, the thing is, I nearly got married some years ago, to a guy called Jimmy,' she said, bracing herself in case the mention of his name jogged Caleb's memory, but he didn't react, just looked at her with interest. 'And I needed some time on my own after the relationship finished to get my head straight and then I got so busy at work I let things drift,' she said.

'Why did you split up with him?' he asked brusquely.

She sighed, feeling the old familiar tug of guilt in her chest. 'I changed my mind about whether he was the right guy for me and called the wedding off at the last minute.'

He blinked, but his expression remained impassive. 'Do you regret it now?'

'No. It was the right decision. It wouldn't have worked out. He was a really nice guy, but being married to Jimmy would have stifled me in the end, killed my spirit.'

Caleb nodded as if he understood exactly what she was talking about.

'I think I felt the same about my ex-fiancée,' he said, surprising her with his direct honesty.

'She was a beautiful woman, incredibly smart and very driven, but there was something missing for me. I thought for a long while that it wouldn't matter, but as soon as we started to talk seriously about arranging the wedding it became apparent it wasn't going to work for me. There was something else wrong too, but I can't remember what it was.' He squeezed his eyes shut as if trying to bring the memory to the fore.

Don't let this be the moment when he remembers everything, she prayed silently—

not when they were just starting to get on so well.

'I think my problem's always been that I was brought up by two parents who argued all the time and I found my life growing up incredibly stressful,' she jumped in, hoping to divert his attention back to her story in order to impart the whole sorry tale, just in case she found herself suddenly talking to the pre-accident Caleb—who she was sure wouldn't be quite so interested in her reasons for letting him down so badly in the past.

'They seemed to be on the verge of divorce all the time and I hated it. It made me so anxious I used to lock myself in my bedroom and turn my music up really loud so I didn't have to hear the constant bickering. It made me crave stability, so when I met Jimmy a year before I left for university I thought he was the perfect person to give me what I needed.'

Caleb just looked at her as if to tell her to carry on, so she continued.

'He was such a calm and well-balanced person—the embodiment of a safe, solid future in my mind. Exactly the sort of man

I wanted to settle down with. The complete opposite of my dad.'

And you, *Caleb.*

She cleared her throat nervously. 'Somehow the relationship survived through our time at separate universities—with a small blip—' She glanced at him then hurried on, 'And he proposed to me a couple of years after we graduated.'

It was nearing midday now and the sun was out in full force. Elena was beginning to feel increasingly stifled in her suit so she slipped her jacket off, looping it over her arm to carry it instead.

'I thought I wanted a relationship like that at the time, but as it got closer to our wedding day this strange kind of panic engulfed me. I was terrified I was heading for a life of middling satisfaction and settling for someone I didn't feel any true passion for. I loved him, but I realised it was only as a friend.'

And she knew this because she knew what real passion felt like. After meeting Caleb at university her feelings for him had crept up on her, day by day, until she could barely see straight with confusion. She'd wanted him, so much, but the sensible side of her brain had told her that Jimmy was a much better bet for a future partner. Caleb was fierce and impulsive and somewhat wild: the kind of man who scared her with his dominating intensity and passion, not to mention his overwhelming sex appeal.

Something that was still powerfully evident today.

'I hurt Jimmy really badly and I still feel awful about it, but it was for the best. He's fine now. He met someone else and they've just had a little girl. I hear they're getting married next year.'

When she finally turned to look at him again, Caleb was nodding thoughtfully as if he understood where she was coming from.

They'd reached her hotel now, which had views from the city's beach across the sparkling blue of the Balearic Sea.

'It won't take me long to grab my bag; I'm on the first floor.'

To her surprise, he followed her to the lift.

Shrugging off a twist of nerves, she pressed the button and waited for the lift to arrive.

She guessed he was following her mandate to keep him in her sights at all times to the absolute letter.

Typical Caleb.

Once up on her corridor it took her three attempts to make her key card work in her door and she finally stumbled into the room, flushed in the face and her skin prickling with awareness as Caleb followed her inside.

'Okay, I'll just be a minute. I need to grab my things from the bathroom and wardrobe then we can go.'

He just nodded, watching her as she shoved her meagre possessions into her suitcase then struged to zip it up.

'Here, let me do that,' he said, putting his hands on her shoulders and gently but firmly guiding her out of the way so he could get to the case.

She saw him wince with pain as his cracked rib protested when he bent down and started tugging at the zip.

'Caleb, stop! I can do it.'

Without thinking, she pressed her hand against his chest, feeling the dips and peaks of his muscles shift under her touch as he tensed with surprise.

It suddenly felt too seductive in that small room—the two of them standing so close together, only inches away from the bed. She could feel the heat from his body throbbing against the palm of her hand and his enticing scent flooded her nose, making her senses reel.

When she looked up into his face he was gazing at her with such intensity in his eyes she thought she might melt under the heat of it.

Little shivers of excitement raced over her skin and she drew in a shaky breath, feeling her blood pulse thickly through her veins.

No, no, no, this shouldn't be happening. She shouldn't be looking at the full firmness of his mouth and thinking how wonderful it would be to feel it on hers again, or about how much she wanted the comforting strength of his arms around her, or how she longed for him to guide her over to the bed and lay her down, trapping her underneath him so she could experience the feeling of their bodies pressed closely together.

She shouldn't be wanting all that.

But she was. She was.

Denying herself was almost too much to bear.

But she *had* to.

Withdrawing her hand from where it still lay over his heart, she forced her mouth into a wobbly smile.

'I don't want you in pain because of me,' she muttered, the tormenting subtext of the words not lost on her.

He frowned, his eyes dark with confusion.

'Let's get out of here,' she mumbled, turning away and hurriedly zipping up the final side of the case, not daring to look at him again in case he saw how much she ached for him to touch her reflected in her expression.

They didn't say a word to each other as they left the room and walked side by side down the corridor and into the lift, the air around them throbbing with a strange new tension.

Once back on the street, Elena stood blinking in the bright afternoon sunlight feeling as if they'd moved into some kind of parallel universe up there in the hotel room.

'Let's grab a bite to eat from that café

on the beach,' Caleb said, pointing to the place in question, his voice sounding a little rough.

'Okay, sure. I could eat,' Elena said, deciding the best thing to do was just pretend the incident in the hotel had never happened. That was the only way she was possibly going to get through the next twenty-four hours.

After locating a suitable table, she watched him stroll over to the counter and place their order for food and coffee. The woman serving him gave him a coquettish grin and leant forward in a seductive manner to ask him a question and Elena experienced a pinch of jealousy as she saw him return her smile.

She put her hand over her heart where it hurt the most and gave a gentle rub there.

Oh, no.

She was in such trouble.

He returned a minute later, balancing a couple of plates of food in one hand and grasping the handles of two mugs of coffee in the other.

'Here, let me help you,' Elena said, rising to take the plates from him so he could put the mugs down on the table without spilling the hot liquid everywhere.

She was horrified to find her hands were shaking and sat down quickly, placing them in her lap before he noticed.

When she looked up to say thanks for the drink he'd put in front of her she saw he was frowning, as if something was bothering him.

'Did we spend a lot of time together at university?' he asked.

The memory of her and Caleb sharing a bottle of wine in his room after a study session flitted across her vision, stealing her breath away. It had been on that night that everything had changed between them.

That fateful night, in a drunken haze, when she'd admitted her true feelings for him and he'd dragged her into his arms and kissed her, making her insides melt and her blood fizz with excitement.

Forcing herself to unclench her now sweaty hands, she gave him as composed a smile as she could muster.

'Yes, we were pretty close back then. We were doing the same course so we had a lot in common. Our tutor put us together as partners on a project at the beginning of the first term and found we worked well together.'

The memory of her broken promise to Caleb that she'd return to university after the Christmas holidays a free woman after breaking up with Jimmy, ready to commit her newly unchained heart to him, pressed heavily on her.

Picking up her drink to give her restless hands something to do, she took a tentative sip of the hot liquid.

'So why haven't we seen each other for so long?' Caleb asked, the look in his eyes so searching she choked on her drink.

'Are you okay?' he asked with amusement in his voice as he reached over to pat her gently on the back.

'I'm fine,' she gasped, taking the opportunity to wipe her eyes with the napkin that had come with the sandwich so she didn't need to look at him while she answered.

'I guess life just got in the way. We've both been so focused on our careers.'

When she finally looked up at him again he nodded slowly. 'Tell me more about our time together at university,' he said, giving her the impression that he needed to hear about it to help him understand something.

So she did. She told him about the way they'd met on the first day of term and how grumpy he'd been with her when their tutor had paired them up.

'I was so annoyed with you I gave you a real dressing-down at the end of that lesson. I think I said something about how just because I was a woman it didn't mean I couldn't beat your arrogant arse at engineering.' She smiled at the memory, remembering how it had taken a lot of guts to say that to him, and how proud she was of herself afterwards that she hadn't let him just walk all over her.

He'd been taken aback by her defensiveness at first, but once he realised she meant every word he'd challenged her to a quiz on engineering terms.

'And I won,' she told him, smiling at his raised eyebrow. 'But you were a good loser. You just gave me this respectful kind of nod and then offered to take me to the nearest pub to toast my win. We ended up staying there all night and by the end of it we were firm friends.'

He snorted with laughter, clearly amused by this, though the expression on his face told her he was impressed by what she was telling him.

'We spent a lot of time together after that,' she continued, warming to her theme now, 'and talked about a lot of personal stuff too, especially the things we found tough growing up. Like you being brought up in a single-parent household and being bullied at school, and me living with parents that constantly rowed or sniped at each other. I think we felt a certain kind of affinity with each other after that.'

He continued to look at her with a frown pinching his brow now, but didn't comment. Clearly he had no memory of any of that.

'We liked the same kind of movies too—sci-fi and fantasy,' she said, to fill the silence that had fallen between them.

He nodded in agreement, a relieved sort of smile playing about his mouth as if this made total sense to him.

'Most of our other friends weren't interested in them so we often went to the cinema together to see them and stay up late dissecting them afterwards.' She smiled, trying to hide how sad those memories made her feel now. 'Good times.'

'It sounds like we had fun together,' he murmured, his eyes never leaving hers.

She gazed back at him, remembering how happy they'd both been then, how full of vigour and positivity and excitement for the future—a future she'd hoped would have him in it in some way—and felt her spirits plummet. Would he have been a happier, less angry man today if they'd stayed together then?

'We did,' she said quietly, swallowing past the lump in her throat.

He opened his mouth to ask her something else but, before he could get the words out, his mobile began to ring, mercifully diverting his attention away from her rapidly heating face.

'That was Benita,' he said once he'd concluded the call and put his mobile down on the table. 'She managed to get hold of Carter. He's agreed to meet for dinner tonight and, as we anticipated, he's bringing his wife with him.'

He raised both eyebrows. 'Looks like we're on, girlfriend.'

She covered a resurgence of nerves with a smile. 'Great.'

Once they'd polished off their food, at Elena's request they spent the walk back to his apartment going over any relevant points about Araya Industries that might come up in conversation with the Americans, making sure she was fully briefed—or at least as much as a girlfriend working in the same industry might be.

It was fascinating to hear how he'd chosen to run his business, but Elena experienced a twinge of guilt at being trusted with detailed strategies and projections when Caleb had been so keen not to allow her anywhere near his business operation only the day before.

This was all to help him though, she reminded herself firmly. She wasn't going to take advantage of it at any point.

'So tell me about your business,' he said once they'd covered all the salient points about his.

His question caught her off guard and she stumbled a little, feeling him grab her elbow to right her, and gave him a strained smile.

'Er…well, I run a company in England

called Zipabout. We make single-person electric vehicles to be used for short trips around towns and cities.'

He raised his eyebrows with interest. 'And what sort of battery are you using to power them?'

She thought about telling him the truth, somehow bringing the conversation round to the fact she was hoping his company would be the one to supply it, but her conscience wouldn't let her. It would be totally inappropriate to mention it when he didn't remember the row they'd already had about it.

With a sinking heart she said, 'We're looking into that at the moment. I have a few leads.'

Darn, darn, darn! And it could have been such a good opportunity to find out whether he'd be interested in supplying his battery to her without the angst and anger from their past getting in the way. But it was too much of a morally ambiguous move for her to do that.

Caleb was nodding slowly, looking as though he was going to ask something else, and she held her breath, poised to fudge an answer, but, as luck would have it, at that moment his attention was diverted as he looked round to fully take in their surroundings and said, 'We need to take this turn for my apartment.'

It was just the distraction she needed in order to redirect the topic of conversation without it seeming strange.

'So how long have you lived on this street?' she asked, waving her hands around expansively. 'It's a lovely area.'

As they walked out onto his street, with him telling her he'd been here for the last four years and how he came to find it, it suddenly struck her how businesslike the area was. The apartments were large and expensive-looking, but didn't give the impression of being held together by a cohesive community. It was a district for people who liked to live alone within a bustling major city.

It made her spirits sink to think of Caleb like that. But then he'd always been fiercely independent and protective of his personal space and she guessed this was just a grown-up extension of that, she reminded herself.

As soon as they walked into his apartment she excused herself, saying she needed a rest before they went out for dinner, in desperate need of some space away from him in order to regroup before their meeting tonight.

Shutting her bedroom door firmly behind her, she took the opportunity to check her email. Her stomach lurched as she saw a message from her Sales Director asking her how it was going with Caleb and checking whether there was any news about being able to use his battery in their car yet.

Closing the laptop with a snap, she resolved not to look at her messages again until after the meal this evening. She was going to need her wits about her tonight, not only for the sake of Caleb's business but also in order to keep her cool whilst looking as though she was intimately acquainted with the man. He already turned her insides to goo every time he so much as looked at her and if he was going to be touching her all night too she was going to need every ounce of strength she had to remain unflustered and in control. The last thing she wanted was for Caleb to suspect she was enjoying his company as more than a friend.

That was a complication neither of them needed at the moment.

CHAPTER SIX

CALEB TOOK A long shower, feeling ener-
gised by the time he'd spent getting to know
a bit more about Elena today.

The intense moment they'd shared in the
hotel room, where the air had positively
crackled between them, had convinced him
that there had to have been more between
them than just friendship during their time
at university.

Judging by her jumpiness around him
afterwards, she'd definitely felt the same
weight of possibility that had hummed between them as they stood gazing at each
other with her hand pressed against his heart.

Having the space to think about it now,
he realised he'd been aware of an odd kind
of tension between them all day, as if she
was trying to suppress something—or hide
something, maybe. Had they not taken their

relationship further because she'd been seeing that Jimmy guy? Had he, Caleb, been the blip she'd mentioned?

Perhaps this connection he felt had always been there, but even though they were both single now Elena didn't think it appropriate to act on it when he was just out of hospital after the accident.

Well, to hell with that. Why should a bang on the head stop them from exploring this thing between them? He wasn't an invalid. He knew his own mind.

Pulling on a smart shirt and trousers for dinner with a determination to find out whether he was right later, he walked out into the living area to discover Elena was also dressed for their meeting and was waiting for him.

The pale pink dress she had on was beautifully understated but entirely beguiling at the same time. It had a halter top, which tied behind her long, elegant neck and showcased her pale, slender shoulders. He couldn't help but notice how the bodice of the dress dipped in under her full breasts then gently curved against her slender waist, perfectly emphasising her hourglass figure.

Feeling her watching him, he dropped his gaze to look at the skirt instead, which was slim-fitting and narrowed at the knee, making her legs look as if they went on for miles.

Forcing himself to snap his mouth shut and pull his gaze up to her face, he gave her a nod of hello and went into the kitchen to get himself a very cold drink of water.

Right now wasn't the time to explore his theory. He had more immediate things to deal with, in the shape of persuading Jonathan Carter to take his business.

'Will you be ready to go in five minutes?' he asked, placing the glass carefully into the sink with an unsteady hand.

'I'm ready when you are,' she replied, but he could have sworn he saw a flash of concern on her face. Perhaps she was nervous about the charade they were about to embark on. It suddenly occurred to him that every time Elena saw him after a break she seemed a little more tense, as if she was expecting him to do or say something she was afraid of. But why?

He remembered with a jolt that she'd mentioned at the hospital that they'd had a row right before his accident, but in his befuddled state he'd not asked her what it had been about.

'Elena?'

She looked round at him as she went to grab her handbag from the table by the door.

'What did we argue about before my accident?'

Her face seemed to blanch a little.

'Er…' Wrapping her arms around her body, she fixed him with an awkward smile. 'It was an old argument from when we were at university. I don't think it's a good idea for us to talk about it now though. We need to be totally focused on the meeting.' She looked so stricken he decided not to push it any further. Especially when she was doing him such a favour by attending this meeting with him.

But why was she so tense? Perhaps she was still feeling responsible for him being hit by that bike. He wished, not for the first time, that he could remember it.

'Fair enough,' he said, 'but, whatever it was, stop worrying that I'm going to bite your head off every time I see you. We're friends after all.'

'Uh-huh,' she mumbled, not looking at him now.

Walking slowly over to where she stood, he put his hand on her bare arm and felt her quiver under his touch.

She took a quick step away, breaking their contact and folding her arms across her chest.

'We should go. We don't want to be late.'

'Of course,' he said, forcing himself to remain where he was and not touch her again, just to see what she'd do. The urge to provoke more of a reaction was intoxicating.

Grabbing his warm weather overcoat, he slid his arms carefully into the sleeves. He was going to have to be careful not to let Carter see he'd been in an accident or it might serve as another mark against him, especially if the man thought he was in any way mentally incapacitated as well at the moment.

It was funny but refusing to show any physical weakness felt like something he was well acquainted with, but he couldn't quite put his finger on why. It eluded him, like something flittering on the edge of his vision. He knew something important was there, but he couldn't fully grasp what he was looking at.

Damn memory—it was playing havoc with his self-assurance.

But it would all be okay; he'd make sure it was.

As for Elena, he'd get the full story from her eventually, but for now she was right—he needed to keep his head in the game.

The restaurant that Benita had booked them into was on a small, winding side street off the famous grand La Rambla, a tree-lined pedestrian mall in the oldest part of the city.

On Elena's request, the car that Caleb had ordered dropped them in the Plaça de Catalunya, next to the magnificent fountain and the looming Francesc Macià monument—that looked to Elena a bit like an upside-down staircase—so they could soak up the buzzy atmosphere on their way to the restaurant.

They walked together, close but not touching, along the busy street bustling with tourists and locals alike, then detoured down one of the small side streets and through a labyrinth of roads crowded on both sides with a mixture of brightly lit pavement cafés, designer clothes shops and trinket stalls, until they reached the Gothic Quarter, where their final destination was located.

According to Caleb, El Gótico had served its famous fusion of Spanish and Mediterranean fare for the past ten years and was a favourite with Barcelonans, as well as the handful of tourists that occasionally stumbled across it.

The décor was a mixture of warm, earthy colours with rustic wooden furniture and a tiled terracotta floor which contrasted sharply with the angular metal and glass of the staircase and bar. Bright splashes of primary colours were picked out on the back wall, which were also reflected in the small lamps and glass water carafes on each table, giving the place the impression of chic modernism. The whole effect was both comforting and uplifting.

The delicious smell of the place wrapped around Elena's senses, making her mouth water as they made their way to the bar, where the greeter stood waiting to welcome them.

Caleb spoke to the woman in rapid Spanish and a moment later they were whisked towards the staircase leading to the upper mezzanine of the restaurant, which had a long glass balcony affording diners views of the lamplit tables below.

Just as he was about to mount the stairs, Elena put her hand on Caleb's arm to stop him. She wanted to make sure they made the most of this opportunity to charm the Americans and for that to happen Caleb was going to have to rein in his more dominating side for a while.

'I'm sure I don't need to say this, but go easy on the man tonight, okay? Just until everyone's had a chance to find their feet here.'

Caleb's eyebrow shot up. 'You think I'm going to dangle him from the balcony if he doesn't agree to a partnership?'

She batted a hand at him, suppressing a smile. 'No, of course not. But I know you; you'll want to go in all guns blazing. I recommend a lighter touch. If he's here with his wife he's not going to take too kindly to being bullied and harangued.'

'I wouldn't—'

She put up a hand to pre-empt his angry rebuttal. 'Not intentionally, I know, but you can come across as a little bit abrasive and intimidating until someone gets to know you. Show him a bit of your soft side too, that's my advice.'

Caleb blinked at her, his brows drawn into a tight frown as he appeared to consider what she'd said. After a moment he nodded slowly, his frustrated expression clearing and being replaced with a wolfish grin. There was something else in his eyes too that made her tummy flip and her blood begin to race. She stared at his mouth, wondering erratically how she would react if he leant forwards and kissed her right now.

'Okay, I'll be nice,' he murmured.

Shoving away her lustful urges, she nodded. 'Good.' She let out a gasp of surprise as he suddenly slipped his hand around her back and drew her closer to him.

'Just relax, *cariño*. You seem tense and that's going to look strange to our guests.'

Swallowing hard, she gave him a jerky nod, her heart banging hard against her chest and her nerves jangling due to their intimate proximity.

'Perhaps I should practice my soft side on

you before they get here,' he murmured, his dark eyes boring into hers.

'How are you going to do that?' she asked, but before she could draw breath he leant in towards her and brushed his mouth against hers.

Fireworks seemed to go off deep inside her body and she wondered wildly for a second how the other diners would react if she suddenly burst into flames in front of them.

Caleb's lips were warm and firm, his mouth fitting perfectly with hers. She stood frozen to the spot, too befuddled to react, as a crazy surge of desire unfolded deep inside her, spiralling out to the very ends of her fingers and toes.

His hands slid into her hair and instinctively she sank against him, her body craving the hard press of his against it.

A moment later she was left gasping for air when he drew away from her, giving her a strange knowing kind of smile and nodding towards the upper mezzanine, his arm pressing into her back as he encouraged her to mount the staircase with him.

'Let's go and find our seats, ready for the show,' he murmured into her ear, his breath tickling the sensitive skin on her exposed neck and making her shiver with longing.

Oh, goodness, it was going to be impossible to keep her cool if he was going to be this physically attentive all evening.

Somehow she managed to make it up the stairs on rather wobbly legs and had just settled herself into a chair that Caleb held out for her when Carter and his wife arrived and she had to stand up again to greet them.

In a fit of continued nerves at Caleb's proximity, Elena managed to knock her knife onto the floor, which then skidded under the table, causing a flurry of amused response as they all tried to locate it so she could retrieve it, apologising profusely as she did so, which fortuitously broke what could have been an icy start to the meeting.

There was something so healthy and vibrant about the couple, Elena thought dazedly as she smiled a more composed hello to them once she'd straightened up after her little mishap. She guessed that was what people who had incredible wealth and an inclination to take care of themselves looked like—polished and dauntingly self-assured. They put Elena in mind of

a high-powered couple from the eighties'
American soap operas she used to watch
for guilty pleasure late at night during her
university days.

Mrs Carter, who must have been in her
early fifties, wore a flattering shift dress
with wide shoulders and her hair was so
coiffed it looked as though every strand
had been sprayed separately into place. Mr
Carter, who looked to be of a similar age,
was just as polished in a dark grey double-
breasted suit and blindingly white shirt to
match his blindingly white teeth.

Caleb took the lead by holding out his
hand for them to shake and introducing
Elena as his girlfriend—which only added
to the fluttering sensation in the pit of her
stomach—then gesturing for them all to
take a seat.

The atmosphere was a little awkward at
first; Mr Carter appeared to be on the defen-
sive, as if waiting for Caleb to become angry
about the fact he was considering walking
away from the partnership they'd been discussing, but after a few minutes of attentive
questions from Caleb about how he and his
wife liked Barcelona and being given a few

pointers on the places they must visit whilst here, he appeared to relax a little.

The waiter came over and they ordered a bottle of local wine and a selection of food for the table on Caleb's recommendation and the conversation turned to business.

At first Elena sat back, drinking her wine a little too fast and watching Caleb lead the discussion with something close to awe. She found his clear handle on the market and technical, as well as fiscal, knowledge truly breathtaking and he seemed to be impressing Carter too, because the man was actually sitting back in his seat now and had taken his hand off his wife's lap, where they'd been holding hands.

Putting down her glass, Elena gave the woman a smile and was rewarded with a genuinely warm grin back.

'So how long have you two been together?' Brie Carter asked her with an inquisitive glint in her eye as the two men expounded on the state of the rechargeable battery market in the States.

Elena's stomach lurched. 'Er...well, we've known each other since we met at Cambridge. Caleb was doing an Erasmus exchange year and we became good friends.'

'And that turned into more, I see,' Brie said with a hint of a plea for some juicy gossip to break up the work talk.

Elena glanced at Caleb to check whether he was listening, but he seemed to be deep in conversation with Jonathan Carter. Taking another large gulp of her wine and feeling its warming effect steady her nerves, she leant forward in her chair and said, 'To be honest, it was a love-hate relationship for a long while, but we met again recently and worked things out and we're a strong couple now.'

'I guess that's what makes powerful men so exciting to be with,' Brie said with a glimmer of recognition in her eyes. 'The unpredictability of them.'

Elena smiled. 'Yes, I've always had trouble working Caleb out. He keeps his emotions close to his chest and can come across as a bit of a prickly character, but he's actually an intensely kind, passionate and caring man.'

It wasn't just the alcohol warming her veins now, but also the recognition of the truth in her words. She'd never met anyone else like Caleb and she suspected she never would again. He was one of a kind.

'That's good to hear,' Brie said with a thoughtful nod.

Sensing an advantage in convincing Carter's wife about Caleb's suitability for a working relationship with her husband, she took the opportunity to endorse him some more.

'He's the most brilliant, focused and hard-working person I've ever met and he'll be the best business partner your husband's ever had,' she said, throwing the older woman a conspiratorial smile. 'He never fails to excite and inspire me, both in a business sense and on a personal level. Always has.'

She felt Caleb shift next to her as he slid his arm across her back to rest gently on her shoulders. She nearly jumped out of her seat as she felt his fingers brush against the exposed skin of her upper arm, sending little electric currents rushing across her nerve endings. Turning her head, she saw he was looking at her with that dark intensity in his gaze again and her cheeks flooded with heat as panic rose in her chest. Had he heard what she'd just said about him?

If so, did he realise she was telling the truth and not just putting on an act for the Americans?

But his expression gave nothing away, his attention seemingly focused on the complex business discussion he was involved in as he asked her to qualify an answer to something about the market for rechargeable batteries in the UK. She forced herself to relax her rigid posture and answer as clearly and succinctly as possible while her pulse raced and her palms grew hot with worry that he'd overheard her gushing admiration of him.

But when she'd finished he nodded his thanks, removed his arm and turned back to Carter, as if he'd not noticed a thing.

It seemed he hadn't heard what she'd said about him and he was just playing the part of attentive boyfriend.

Thank goodness.

It could put them both in a really difficult position if he knew how she really felt about him, especially as their relationship was such a tangled mess. Her stomach lurched as she allowed herself to consider how it might feel to pursue a real relationship with him. It was a disconcerting yet also unnervingly exciting idea, but she'd be a fool to even entertain it. She'd come to Barcelona in the hopes of being his partner in business only—which, of course, she'd thoroughly messed up—and to hope, even for a second, that anything of a romantic nature might develop with Caleb now, when he couldn't remember what had happened between them, was completely reprehensible.

Pushing the notion to the back of her mind, she made sure to keep the conversation focused on Brie after that and they spent the rest of the meal chatting happily about her daughters and the wedding that she was helping to plan, which was taking place in Boston that August.

Elena tried her best to concentrate on what Brie was saying but she couldn't help but tune in to what Caleb and Jonathan were discussing, especially when their voices became more animated. Thankfully, it seemed it was just friendly rivalry, and the two men became more and more relaxed with each other as more wine was consumed and the evening wore on.

Despite her worry about Caleb struggling due to his head injury, he'd coped admirably with the questions that Carter fired at him. It seemed he'd done it; he'd kept his cool and turned the American's opinion of him around. In fact, to Elena's delight and relief, he appeared to have returned to the man she remembered knowing all those years ago at university.

The idea of it made her heart flutter.

She'd become increasingly aware of him sitting only inches away from her throughout the end of the meal, his heady, clean scent in her nose and the heat from his body warming her side, so it was something of a relief to her addled senses when Jonathan pronounced it time for them to go back to their hotel.

The four of them stood and the two men shook hands firmly, Carter's initial wariness nowhere to be seen now as he clapped Caleb jovially on the back.

'Good to meet you, Caleb. I'll get my team to contact you about moving forward with this partnership as soon as we get back to the States.'

Brie leaned in to give Elena an elegant air-kiss near each cheek, then drew her close on the pretext of giving her a hug to whisper in her ear. 'It's wonderful to see how Caleb inspires such genuine loyalty in you. I can tell by the way you look at him how much you care about him.'

She drew back to look Elena in the eye. 'It's heartening to see, especially after the rumours we've heard about what a hard character he is to get on with,' she murmured. 'But, after meeting the two of you tonight, I sincerely think my husband's going to find working with him a positive experience.'

Jonathan Carter turned from listening to Caleb's assurances he'd be primed for the next point of contact to give Elena a dazzling smile. 'It was wonderful to meet you too, Elena. Caleb here's a lucky man.' He slapped Caleb on the back again and Elena had to hide her frown of concern when she noticed him wincing in pain from his injured rib.

'Thank you for preventing my wife from dying of boredom with all our business talk,' Carter went on, not seeming to notice Caleb's physical discomfort. 'It looked like the two of you had a lot in common, no doubt swapping tales about the two of us!' he boomed, gesturing between himself and Caleb, then sliding his arm around his wife's waist and giving her a hard squeeze which made her gasp and slap him gently on the chest in retaliation.

Elena's breath caught in her throat as she felt Caleb slide his arm around her waist and pull her closer to him, as if wanting to mirror the American's loving behaviour.

As part of the act, Elena reminded herself fuzzily.

Heart thumping in her throat, she watched the couple as they weaved away through the tables towards the stairs leading to the ground floor, then carefully extricated herself from Caleb's hold on the pretence of grabbing her jacket from the back of her chair.

'Well, that went well, I think,' she said, looking up into Caleb's face to find him frowning, as if perplexed about something.

Because she'd moved away from him so deliberately?

Probably.

She felt pretty sure he wasn't used to women rejecting his touch.

It made her wonder again whether he'd heard her gushing praise of him.

'You did a great job, Caleb; it sounds like a partnership is in the bag,' she said, shrugging her jacket on awkwardly. She couldn't quite look him in the eye now. Not after she'd seen the way he was looking at her a moment ago.

As much as she wanted him to know she was sorry for the way she'd treated him in the past and wanted to make amends, she also didn't want to give him the wrong impression here tonight.

She needed to be more careful.

'Yes, he seemed to be on board,' Caleb said, his voice a low, seductive rumble that sent a shiver of unwelcome longing down her spine.

'Shall we go?' she asked, her voice sounding prim and strained as she overcompensated for her body's inappropriate reaction.

'Sure. Lead the way,' he said, gesturing for her to leave first, with a somewhat unnerving glint in his eyes.

As they walked away from the Gothic quarter, Caleb finally allowed himself to think about what he'd overheard Elena saying to Carter's wife about him.

She could have just been playing the game of being his lover, of course, but there had been something in the way she'd said it that had made his breath catch in his throat. Clearly she'd thought he wasn't listening because when he'd turned to catch her eye she'd looked almost—shifty.

So there *was* something more than friendship between them, just as he'd suspected. But if that was the case, why was she pretending that there wasn't?

He had no idea.

What he did know was that he was going to make sure to find out before she left for England and do everything in his power to smooth things over with her.

The kiss they'd shared before Carter and his wife had arrived had made his body hum with tension all evening. When he'd seen the look of concern on her face he'd wanted to do something to reassure her he was going to do whatever it took to win the Americans over, but as soon as his mouth had met hers he'd been lost in a great surge of hunger for her. The sounds and sights of the restaurant had faded away until all he was aware of was the gentle sway and press of Elena's body against his and the sweet, exotic fragrance of her. Her mouth had felt so good against his it had taken a monumental effort to drag himself away from her and not grab her hand and run with her out of the restaurant and jump into the next cab to take them home.

After that, watching her charming Carter's wife and dazzling the couple with her wit, intelligence and profound beauty—he'd found it almost impossible to keep his mind solely on the business conversation.

Throughout the entire evening he'd been intensely aware of the connection between them, taut and alive, as if it was a tangible thing drawing them ever closer together.

He wanted to know more about what was going on between them—*had* to know, for the sake of his sanity.

Yes, he assured himself, he wasn't going to let her go until he'd got the full measure of Elena Jones.

CHAPTER SEVEN

THE CAR PICKED them up a couple of streets away from the restaurant and took them straight home to Caleb's apartment, the two of them sitting in a buzzing, tension-filled silence as they looked out at the wide city streets flashing by.

'You were great tonight,' Caleb said after his driver had pulled up outside his building and he'd helped Elena out of the car, feeling her cool, small hand in his and marvelling at how good it felt to have it there. 'Carter's wife really seemed to like you.'

She flashed him an equable smile as she straightened up. 'I liked her; she was a really lovely woman, very focused on her family.'

'Well, I owe you big for what you did for me tonight.'

There was a loaded moment where they stood and looked at each other, the gentle, far-off sounds of the city at night making him feel as though they were trapped in a bubble together. Caleb broke the strange energy by smiling and saying, 'Anyway, thanks, Elena. I really appreciate your help.'

She shuffled a little on the spot and nodded, her bright eyes gleaming in the light thrown out from the streetlight above them.

'It was my pleasure. Anything for a friend.'

The emphasis she put on the word 'friend' made him bristle.

It suddenly struck him that by tomorrow her forty-eight hours of observation of him would be up and she might well leave and return to England.

And he found he really didn't want her to go.

He wondered where this intense need to keep her here longer had sprung from. Okay, he found her really attractive and was impressed with her business acumen and how smart and savvy she was, but he never normally felt this sort of draw to a woman.

There was something different about her, something *compulsive*.

He had to explore what this thing was between them, or it would haunt him for ever.

Turning back to look into her hooded eyes, he was intrigued to see she seemed to be having her own non-verbal debate with herself. Was she only holding back because she thought he was still incapacitated? *Weak?* Frustration surged through him. Well, he wasn't. He was completely in his right mind and he knew damn well what he wanted—her, and now.

Pulling his key card out of his pocket, he let them into his building and they stepped into the lift that would take them up to his apartment, Elena swaying gently in her heels beside him.

Being around her felt *right*, dammit—as if she were a missing link in his life.

And he was going to do whatever it took to have her back in it.

'Elena?' he said, turning to face her once the lift had begun its smooth ascent.

'I know what happened between us at university. I know we were more than just friends. And I know we didn't act on it because of Jimmy.'

Elena swallowed hard as blood rushed to her head and her stomach did a backflip.

His memory had finally returned.

'You remember?' she whispered through lips that would barely form the words.

He nodded, his beautiful mouth curving into another of its wolfish, dangerous smiles.

The lift came to an abrupt stop, making her stomach do an extra flip for good measure. She could barely breathe with worry about what he was going to say now he remembered what had happened all those years ago. Would he be angry with her? Shout and swear at her, or just be coldly dismissive again?

Her pulse throbbed in her head. She really hoped he wouldn't go ballistic and chuck her out on the street now, not after what they'd just been through together. Not now she'd finally met the real Caleb again. She couldn't bear it.

The door of the lift swished open and he strode out and straight over to his door without another word, slipping the key into the lock then holding the door open for her to walk through it.

She strode into his apartment with her head held resolutely high, determined to keep her cool, to restate her case and hopefully prove to him once and for all that she was sorry about how their relationship had ended.

Her heart hammered in her chest as she watched him shrug off his jacket and hang it up before finally turning back to face her.

His expression was impassive as his dark gaze bored into hers.

'We've wasted a lot of time leading our separate lives and I think it's time to remedy that.'

She stared at him in shock. Had she misheard? It sounded as though he was talking about pursuing more than friendship with her. 'I'm sorry?' she stuttered, aware that her hands had begun to shake at her sides.

'What happened was a long time ago, and we're both free and single now,' he continued, apparently oblivious to her befuddlement. 'Without anything standing in our way. No partners, no memory loss—'

'Do you remember everything that happened between us?' she asked, her voice sounding shaky with anticipation and hope.

There was a flash of something in his eyes, remembered pain perhaps, but it quickly disappeared. 'Yes.'

'And you forgive me for it?'

He took a deliberate pace towards her and raised his hand to touch her face, smoothing the backs of his long fingers gently over her cheek.

'I'm not going to let some stupid argument from the past get in the way of what we have here—right now. We're good together, you and I. We fit.'

'Caleb—are you sure?' Her voice came out as a low breath of air as sensation rushed over her skin at his touch. Had she really done it? Made up for the hurt she'd caused him in the past? Her spirits soared as the heavy weight of guilt began to lift and she finally felt as though she could breathe properly again.

'Yes, I'm sure,' he said with a conviction she felt deep in her chest.

Letting out a breathy laugh, she said, 'This is all happening so quickly. I don't know what to think—'

'I understand why you might be unsure about restarting something between us,' he murmured, cutting her off. 'We live in different cities, live different lives, but we can work around that.'

She swallowed hard, her thoughts spinning wildly. Could she finally be about to get her Caleb back?

'This would make me happy and I think it would make you happy too—you and me, here together, tonight.' His mouth curved into a seductive smile, making her insides quiver and her heart leap about in her chest.

Heat rose to her face as a strange sort of panic settled in her stomach. Was she ready for this? After all this time, regretting what had happened between them and hoping, wishing she could do something to make it better—that she could go back in time and do it all differently—now that she was actually here in the moment, a moment where her whole life could change, she was afraid. Terrified.

What if it all went wrong again?

'It seems too soon to be jumping into something, especially after your accident—' she hedged.

He shrugged away her concern. 'I'm fine now. You don't need to worry about me any more.' He moved even closer, making the air crackle around her. 'And I thought you were the one who liked to take every positive out of a situation.'

There was no comeback for that.

'I *know* you, Elena.'

'You do?' she asked breathlessly.

'Yes. And I know we still want the same thing.'

The look of desire in his eyes made her whole body shiver with longing.

'And what's that?' she said, knowing exactly what he was going to say, but hoping he wouldn't because then she'd have to make a really difficult decision.

'That you still want me as much as I want you.'

He was so close now, the feel of his soft breath on her skin making her lips tingle with the craving to feel his mouth on hers again. Somewhere in the back of her mind she was aware that she should stop this, draw away and be the sensible one, insist they talk about all that had happened between them first, point out that it was too soon for them to fall into bed together. That she didn't think it was a good idea.

But that would have been a lie. And she wasn't going to lie to him any more.

So instead she said, 'Yes, I want you.'

Before she could qualify that with 'but I still don't know if it's a good idea *right now*' he'd closed the tiny gap between them and pressed his mouth hard to hers.

Her body responded without conscious thought, her lips opening against his to allow his tongue to dip into her mouth, tasting her, possessing her.

Being careful not to crush his broken rib, she pressed herself against him and felt his arms slip tightly around her back, holding her close to him. His strength enveloped her, making her senses reel with pleasure, and she stumbled backwards as he moved forwards, guiding her gently but purposefully towards the corridor where his empty bedroom waited for them.

They reached the bed in a tangle of limbs, with her grabbing at his clothes with a frenzy and a need that took her by surprise.

Elena had never felt so wanted, so worshipped, as Caleb tugged his shirt over his head, not seeming to care that he was ripping buttons off in his haste. She almost stopped when she heard him grunt as his broken rib must have twanged with pain but, before she could say a word, he shook his head and said, 'I'm fine,' grasping the straps tied behind her head to release the halter neck of her dress then tug at the zip so the silky material fell open and glided down to pool at her feet.

'So beautiful,' he muttered as he bent to kiss her again, sliding his hands down her back, tracing the lines of her body with his fingertips and sending her into raptures of ecstasy. Just the feel of his hands on her was enough to make her shudder with joy.

'There's nothing like making up for lost time,' he murmured against her mouth and all she could do was smile and nod in agreement, her brain too fuzzy with lust to help her form anything like intelligible words.

He guided her gently backwards until her legs hit the side of the bed, but she knew she'd have to be the one to lead this because of his injury, so she wrapped her hands around his arms and steered him round so the bed was behind him instead and used the momentum of him being slightly off balance to make him first sit, then lie down. Then she climbed carefully on top of him, kissing him hard and covetously, the sense of finally being allowed to have him back after all these years of yearning for it making her frantic and greedy.

And some time shortly after that her brain shut down completely and all that was left was the feel of their two bodies moving together and sweet, sweet fulfilment.

The next morning Elena woke to find sun pouring in through the large warehouse-sized windows of Caleb's bedroom.

Blinking blearily, it took her a moment for the events of the night before to rush back to her—and remember exactly what had happened between them.

She'd slept with Caleb.

And it had been amazing.

In the heat of the moment, with his mouth on hers and his body pressed so close they'd almost become one, she'd completely lost herself in him, hazily justifying her easy capitulation by telling herself she owed him some happiness, though in truth she knew deep down she'd done it for her own purely selfish reasons. She'd wanted him so much it had caused her physical pain to imagine tearing herself away from him and stopping it.

And it had been such an incredible night, so full of passion and pleasure.

But it all felt like a surreal dream now.

Turning to look at Caleb lying next to her, she felt her insides flutter and heat with pleasure.

In truth, she was still confused about his sudden change in attitude towards her, especially after he'd been so vociferous at their first meeting about not wanting to have anything to do with her again, but she guessed that after helping him turn Carter's opinion of him around he must have felt she'd paid her dues.

Not that she'd done it for that reason alone. She'd wanted him to be successful with the meeting; she could sense how much it meant to him to win the partnership deal and keep his business thriving— the company he'd worked so hard to build from nothing, just like she had with hers. She wanted him to be happy. To be the man she remembered again.

Trying not to think about how precarious the future of her own company still was, she watched him for a while, his eyelids flickering gently in REM sleep and his wide brow smooth now without his regulation frown creasing it.

She'd been happy too last night, happier than she could remember being in a very long time. Because of him. The guilt and regret that had followed her around for so long that it had felt like an intrinsic part of her seemed to have vanished, leaving a strange, yearning ache in its wake. One she hoped to satisfy with something new and positive and exciting.

A relationship with Caleb, perhaps.

Pushing away a strange nervous sensation in her chest, she slid out of bed and went into his en suite bathroom to take a quick shower, lathering herself all over with his zesty-smelling body wash.

The way he'd looked at her last night when they'd arrived back in his apartment had shaken her to her core. There had been such heat in his eyes, a little like the carnal ferocity she'd seen during their first meeting, although this time it had been driven by desire rather than anger.

He'd looked at her like that before—the

night she'd told him how she really felt about him at university—and the impression it had left on her had stayed with her for the rest of her life.

That feeling of being so coveted, so *wanted* was a hard one to forget. She'd craved it over the years, desperately trying to find a way to feel like that again, but she'd not been successful.

Until now.

She knew she was being reckless here, jumping into something so intense with him so quickly, but she was sick and tired of being sensible. It had brought her nothing but pain and stress in the past and it was high time she started being brave and taking some risks with her heart. Otherwise her life would only ever be half lived and what a waste that would be.

After drying herself, she pulled on an oversized towelling robe that she found on the back of the door and padded quietly back over to the bed.

He was lying on his side facing away from her, towards the wall, apparently still asleep if his regular breathing pattern was anything to go by. Moving to stand by his side of the bed, she looked down at him, at his strong, arresting face, with his usually neatly swept back dark hair mussed and falling over his forehead, making him look younger and less fierce.

She jumped in shock as his eyes sprang open and he grabbed for her, wrapping his arm around her legs and pulling her roughly towards him so she lost her balance and toppled onto him with a squeal of surprise. He kissed her hard before rolling her over, so he was on top now, his brow momentarily pinched as he remembered his damaged rib.

'What are you doing, you maniac?' she spluttered, laughing at his self-reproachful grimace.

'Just saying good morning,' he replied, flashing her a grin before he kissed her again so thoroughly it made her toes curl.

'Well, okay then,' she purred, cupping his jaw in her hands, her whole body buzzing with the joy of finding herself in his arms again. 'I'm so glad we're friends again.'

He frowned, looking a little perplexed. 'Friends? Do you do this with all of your friends?' he asked, nuzzling her neck and placing soft, sensuous kisses against her hyper-sensitised skin.

She laughed, then sighed, running her hands into his bedhead hair. 'No, just you.'

Pulling back, he looked straight into her eyes, his gaze unflinching and determined.

'I know you don't need to be here with me any more, but I want you to stay for a bit longer. We should go to Gaudi's Park Güell today. It's an amazing place. I'd like to show it to you.'

'I don't know, Caleb; perhaps you should rest today—'

He held up a hand to cut her off. 'You can't come all the way to Barcelona and not visit all the places of interest.'

'Places of interest? You sound like a tour guide,' she said with a tease in her tone.

'There's no one better than a resident to show you all the best bits of a city,' he said with a seductive lift of his eyebrow. 'I know all its secrets,' he murmured, lifting his hand to trace the line of her jaw and sending little currents of sensation down her throat, which joined with the ones already humming deep inside her body.

She gave him a dazed sort of smile, barely

able to concentrate as he slid the backs of his fingers down her throat, then lower to skim over the swell of her breasts.

'Well, that would be…really…amazing…' she murmured, her voice coming out broken and husky as she struggled to concentrate on forming the words.

Lust twisted her insides as he leant forwards and kissed her hard again. She responded instinctively to his touch, sliding her arms around his back and wriggling closer to him.

Pulling her underneath his strong, hard body, he murmured, 'Okay, but we'll go later. Much, much later.'

They spent the rest of the morning in bed, only getting out of it for a minute to fetch some food from his fridge for lunch, which they ate right there, sitting naked on top of the covers.

'This reminds me of all those meals we ate sitting on my bed whilst working on our project at uni—though of course we were fully clothed for those,' Elena said, grinning at him with one eyebrow raised. 'I found breadcrumbs in my sheets for days after that. Who knows where we'll find them after this.'

She laughed and he smiled back at her, wishing he could remember the time she was reminiscing about. It was getting harder and harder to pretend he knew the stories she relayed without it seeming suspicious that he didn't bring up some of his own recollections.

He felt a little guilty about lying to her last night, but he'd been so sick of her holding back and wasting time when it had been so clear they were destined to end up like this anyway.

Anyway, she seemed much happier now, and if she was happy then so was he.

After they'd finished eating she left the room and returned a few minutes later in a pair of jeans and a loose-fitting, soft pink T-shirt with her hair scraped back into a ponytail, her lips shiny with some kind of clear lipstick that he wanted to kiss off immediately. She didn't need make-up; she was just as beautiful without it.

'Come on, lazybones, get your carcass out of bed. I thought you were going to show me some of your secrets,' she said, giving him a wide grin.

He rolled out of bed with a grunt and stood up. Pulling her towards him, he kissed her until she squealed with pleasure, but she pushed him away when he began to drag her back towards the bed.

'No, no, you said we should go out and I think you're right; we can't spend all day in bed.'

'Why not?' he murmured, thinking it would be more than okay with him. He couldn't get enough of her—the scent of her soft skin, the feel of her strong legs wrapped around him, the little breathy moans she made in his ear as they moved together...

'Caleb, seriously, get dressed so we can go out.'

He shot her a grimace of annoyance. 'Okay, okay, but it won't be as much fun as staying here,' he ground out. 'I have plenty more secrets I could show you right here in the bedroom.'

'Later,' she said with laughter in her voice.

He loved it when she smiled like that—like she couldn't have stopped herself even if she'd wanted to.

* * *

He took her to Palo Alto, an enclosed old manufacturing complex situated a few roads back from the beach, which was like a hidden island of industrial-style buildings festooned with brightly coloured creepers and greenery that had turned it into a wonderful garden oasis. The buildings had all been converted over the years into light, open workshops for businesses focused on regeneration and rehabilitation of the city and beyond.

'No tourists know about it, only the residents of the city,' Caleb told her as they walked through the alleyways between the buildings, soaking up the effervescent but peaceful air of the place. 'I love wandering around here; I find it a really inspiring place to be. You know, Araya Industries started out in one of these workshops so it'll always be a special place for me. It's where I realised my dreams.'

'It's wonderful. Thank you for trusting me—an outsider—' she winked at him '—to see it. I'm honoured,' she said, turning to kiss him next to a cascade of fuchsia flowers and russet-coloured leaves.

Then afterwards, at Elena's request, they took a cab out to the spectacular multicoloured Park Güell, which had been designed by Gaudi. He watched her run her hand along the top of the wave-shaped benches that had been decorated with millions of pieces of brightly patterned broken tiles, enjoying her delight at the eccentricity of the design.

After sitting for a while, looking out over the picturesque views of the city and the fairy tale–style gatehouses that looked as if they could be made from gingerbread and icing, they went down the steps to see the forest of Greek Doric columns underneath, which had been designed to house an old marketplace beneath the plateau of the park.

He watched her as she wound her way through the pillars, tracing her fingers over the smooth stone and gazing up at the colourful cornices on the ceiling, and it hit him that for the first time since he'd seen her in that hospital room she looked truly relaxed.

The idea that he could be responsible for that made him feel heady with pleasure, as if he could deal with anything life threw at him right now, as long as Elena was here with him. She made him feel light and positive, buzzed and excited…and what was that other sensation…?

Happy.

His breath caught in his throat as the word pierced through him.

It was a feeling that had been missing from his life for far too long now. And Elena was the catalyst—because he knew without a doubt that she was his ideal woman—smart, sexy and so beautiful it made his chest ache to look at her.

And then, out of nowhere, something strange happened.

A memory flashed through his mind: of Elena's face, cold and hard with indifference, just before she slammed a door in his face.

It left him winded, gasping to drag air into his lungs again, his head swimming and thick, as though too heavy for his body to hold up. A slow trickle of horror-tinged despair slid sickeningly through him and he had to lean against the nearest pillar to stop himself from sliding to the floor.

A moment later the real Elena was there

next to him, her hands on his shoulders and a look of deep concern on her beautiful face.

'Caleb! Are you okay?'

The face that looked into his now was so different from the one his mind had conjured up a moment ago he felt relief flood through him. Had it just been his subconscious warning him not to get too carried away with what was developing between them? Not to get too close in case it went wrong like all his other relationships had over the last few years?

Well, to hell with that. He wasn't going to let her get away because he was afraid of this thing between them failing. He wouldn't let it.

'I'm fine,' he said, forcing his mouth into a reassuring smile. 'My rib's just giving me a bit of pain, that's all.'

She nodded, still frowning. 'Okay, then let's get out of here. You're probably pushing yourself too hard.'

'I'm fine, Elena,' he growled, annoyed at her fussing around him, not wanting this one small blip to ruin the wonderful day they'd been having.

She seemed to sense the agitation with himself behind his snappiness because she gave him a knowing smile and said, 'Okay, then let's go and get something to eat. I don't know about you but I could eat a horse right now.'

He nodded his agreement, grateful to her for not making a big scene. He didn't want the remainder of their time together marred by his minor ailments.

Pulling her towards him, he placed a firm kiss on her mouth, wanting to prove to her how happy he was to have her here with him and that he hoped there would be much more of it to come.

She kissed him back with a fervour that rocked him to his soul, proving to him the connection he felt to her wasn't one-sided.

They were going to need to have a serious conversation soon about how to make a relationship work when they were living so far away from each other. Because he knew now that was what he wanted.

He so wished he could remember the relationship they'd had when they were younger. Perhaps it would give him more insight into how to solidify their connection now.

That damn accident had been such bad timing—though it had at least prompted her to stay in Spain a bit longer, and in his apartment too, for which he knew he should be very grateful. It had brought them together after all.

It was disconcerting though, not having all that information about her available to him. Still, more things seemed to be coming back to him in dribs and drabs now so perhaps his brain was beginning to heal.

Pushing away his lingering unease, he kissed her once more before taking her hand to lead her out of the park.

It would all be fine once the rest of his memory came back.

CHAPTER EIGHT

THE NEXT MORNING Caleb rolled reluctantly out of bed, leaving a sexily rumpled and tantalisingly warm Elena in it.

'Do you want me to come to the hospital with you?' she murmured sleepily as he strode towards the en suite bathroom for a shower.

He stopped in his tracks and looked back at her. She was smiling at him in that earnest, intent way that always made his heart turn over.

In truth, he loved the idea of spending the whole of the day with her by his side, but he definitely didn't want her coming to the hospital with him just in case something happened there that made it obvious his memory hadn't fully returned yet.

'No, it'll be boring for you. You stay here, or go shopping or sightseeing or something.

I need to go into the office to make sure everything is running smoothly without me but I'll be back here to spend the afternoon with you.'

She gave him a pained look. 'Okay, but don't get caught up in the office and forget the time. You should really be resting at home still.'

He walked back to the bed and sat down on the side of it, brushing a rogue strand of hair away from her forehead. 'I tell you what, why don't you just spend all day naked in my bed—that'll give me all the incentive I need to come home as soon as possible.'

Laughing, she pulled him down for a kiss and he gave in to her demand and kissed her back, pulling the sheet that separated them away and rolling on top of her, telling himself he still had plenty of time to make his appointment.

He was late for his appointment.

Luckily, the doctor was also running late with his last patient so Caleb didn't need to apologise for his tardiness as he strode into the consulting room. The extra time he'd got to spend with Elena would have been totally worth missing the appointment for anyway. He was fine, still a bit blurry about the events in his past, but, as he told the doctor, who looked at him with a mixture of concern and perplexity at his attitude, he didn't care—he was alive and he had a beautiful, compassionate woman waiting for him back at home and that was what mattered.

Life was good.

After being put through some rather over-the-top extensive tests by the consultant and agreeing reluctantly to come back later in the week for additional testing, he finally managed to escape the hospital, intent on dropping in at Araya Industries for the barest of moments to satisfy himself that everything was running well there before heading straight back to Elena's warm smile and comforting embrace.

Striding through Reception, he greeted a couple of the PAs who worked for his colleagues with a smile, both of them blinking at him in surprise before hurriedly returning his cheery salutation.

Up on his floor he found a rather bemused Benita sitting at her desk outside his office, and he flashed her a smile in greeting then asked her if she could please come in once she'd finished the email she was typing. She stared at him in surprise, also seemingly unnerved by his new jovial attitude, before nodding jerkily, the expression on her face remaining wary as if worried he was just lulling her into a false sense of security before putting the boot in.

Clearly he had a lot of work to do on his people skills.

He'd always been aware that he came across as intense and forthright, but he'd never considered it to be a failing before, too caught up in the running of his business to pay it much mind. Elena's appearance in his life and her bravery in challenging him about it had opened his eyes to it though. It was as if she'd drawn out something that had been buried for far too long within him. With this in mind he made a firm resolution to review the way he dealt with his colleagues in the future.

Sitting down at his desk, he turned on his computer and was just about to look over his email when there was a tentative knock on his door. He called, 'Come in,' and a moment later Benita's head appeared around the door, her face set in a circumspect smile as if she was a little afraid to enter the room in case he was waiting in there to bite her head off.

'Benita, come in,' he said kindly, giving her an encouraging nod.

She shuffled into the room, keeping a good four feet back from the desk where he was sitting.

'How are you feeling?' she asked with trepidation in her voice.

'I'm fine,' he said, wincing inside as he caught the brusqueness in his tone. 'Thanks for asking,' he added and almost laughed at the look of incredulity on her face.

'So, did Carter's people get in contact?' he asked.

She nodded, moving closer to the desk now as if she was beginning to trust his new upbeat attitude. 'I've put the minutes of the Skype meeting onto the DRM and the relevant account managers have been briefed.'

'Good, good,' he said, nodding. 'Thanks.'

She cleared her throat. 'It's good to see you back, Señor Araya. We were worried when we heard about your accident. It looks like your friend took good care of you though.'

'Yes, she did,' he said, the thought of Elena lying naked in his bed waiting for him distracting him for a moment.

'Did you work out your differences about partnering with her business?' Benita asked.

He stared at her like an idiot for a moment, wondering whether his wandering thoughts had somehow made him mix up the words Benita had said to him.

'What did you say?'

She looked a little taken aback, as if she might have put her foot in it. 'I just meant— it seemed as though you were getting on well again—after your meeting didn't go as smoothly as you'd hoped.'

'Our meeting?'

'With Señorita Jones. On the morning before your accident.'

She was looking at him as if she was worried that he'd gone insane.

He batted a hand at her, his thoughts swirling and confused as a strange sinking feeling appeared out of nowhere and slid through his chest. 'Yes, yes, I remember.'

He thought hard for a moment. 'Benita, did you forward me the supporting documents for that meeting?'

'Er…no, you asked me not to. I got the impression you weren't very keen to partner with her company.'

That was strange. Why would he have thought that?

'Well, send them over to me now, will you? I need to take a look at them.'

'Yes, of course.' She paused. 'Is there anything else I can do for you?'

He shook his head, his confusion about what was going on making his brain hurt. 'No, no, that'll be all. Thanks.'

She gave him a nod, then slipped out of the room.

Caleb booted up the DRM programme and clicked on the links that Benita sent through, which connected to a presentation Elena had apparently sent over before a meeting they were meant to be having on Friday.

A meeting he had no memory of.

He read through her proposal with interest, wondering why the hell he'd not jumped at the opportunity she'd put to him.

She needed his battery for her cars and it looked to be a very lucrative deal for both of them.

What was wrong with him? Had he really been so blind or so busy with the American deal that he'd not recognised such a good prospect when she brought it directly to him?

When she'd helped him clinch Carter's business at the meeting the other day he'd been hugely impressed with her knowledge of the industry and her insight into what he did, so much so, he'd made a mental note to look up the company she ran in England, so why had he said no?

He remembered with a sting of conscience that she'd not wanted to discuss the row they'd apparently had right before they'd left for their meeting with the Carters. Had the argument been about him turning the possible partnership between their companies down?

And what had made him do it.

Now he thought about it, whenever he'd pressed her for more information about her business she'd changed the subject. This had surprised him at the time, but he'd written it off as her not wanting to discuss work during her time off.

Or perhaps she'd not wanted to discuss it while she thought he was mentally challenged.

Shutting off his screen, he decided it was time to go home and ask Elena some direct questions before she walked away and went to find someone else to partner with—an idea that filled him with anxiety. After all she'd done for him over the last few days he felt he owed her a debt of gratitude and perhaps this would be the perfect way to repay it.

Walking past Benita's desk, an idea occurred to him.

'Benita, could you book a table at Restaurant Hora for tomorrow night for two people? I know it's Valentine's night,' he said before she could say the words of warning that were clearly on her lips, 'but I know the owner. Just tell him it's for me and he'll find a way to fit us in.'

'Okay, consider it done,' Benita said with a reverential smile, something he'd not seen on her face before. 'Your friend's a lucky lady,' she called as he walked away.

'She is,' he threw back over his shoulder with a wry grin.

Though I think we've moved well past the friends stage now, he thought determinedly to himself as he made to set off home.

His apartment was quiet when he arrived back and he wondered whether she'd decided to go out and sightsee on her own after all, but as he strolled to his bedroom his spirits lifted when he saw she was sitting up naked in his bed with just a pair of glasses perched on her nose, tapping away on her laptop.

She was so absorbed in what she was doing she gave a little start when she finally noticed him standing in the doorway watching her and quickly snapped her laptop shut.

'Did you miss me?' he asked, shedding his clothes and dropping them on the floor as he moved towards her.

The expression in her eyes softened as he climbed onto the bed next to her and she twisted away for a second to put the laptop carefully by the side of the bed before turning back to face him.

He kissed her hard, feeling her sink

against his body as he dragged her closer, the heat and softness of her skin soothing away his tension from being away from her.

'You were only gone a couple of hours,' she chided, but couldn't seem to help herself from smiling and saying, 'but yes, I missed you.'

'Good,' he said, sliding his hands down her body so she made a soft little sighing noise in the back of her throat.

It felt so right having her there in his arms, like nothing he'd ever experienced before. And it wasn't just lust driving that feeling, it was a sense of belonging too. She *belonged* here in his bed. He just needed to find a way to keep her there indefinitely now.

'So, Elena, tell me more about why you need my battery for your car?' he murmured into her hair as she kissed the spot at the back of his jaw that always sent him wild.

Whipping her head back, she looked at him, startled.

'What…er…what do you want to know?' she asked, her expression suddenly guarded.

The wariness in her eyes gave him pause.

'Why are you so jumpy? What aren't you telling me? Every time I've asked questions about your business you've changed the subject.'

Closing her eyes, she let out a long, frustrated sigh, then seemed to give herself a little shake and pull herself together.

'It seemed wrong to discuss business when you weren't well.' She looked down at her fingers, which were plucking nervously at the sheet. 'And the truth is, I didn't give you the full story then about what's going on with it. I was afraid you might see it as a weakness.'

Ah, so, as he'd suspected, there was more to it than she'd initially let on.

'Okay, I'm listening and I promise not to judge.'

She nodded and he saw her swallow hard. 'The truth is, we used to have a supplier who had designed a battery specifically to fit in the car. Initially we wanted to use an English company so we could say the car was fully manufactured in the UK, but very recently they've let us know that there's a fatal flaw with the design of it and they can't figure out how to fix it. So we're in a precarious position now. We have a lot of pre-orders and the shell of the car ready to go, but no battery to power it.'

He frowned, comprehending now why she'd be so panicked. It could be catastrophic for her business if she didn't find a replacement battery.

He nodded, thinking hard. 'Well, from what you've told me, and the documents I looked at today, it seems to me like it could be a mutually beneficial partnership. I don't see why it would be a problem to let you have the battery for your car.'

She stared at him, her eyes wide with surprise. 'What?'

He smiled at her bemusement. 'I'm saying I'd be happy to let your company use my battery in the car.'

To his consternation, instead of flinging herself into his arms with joy she continued to stare at him with a mixture of confusion and reticence. 'I don't know if that's a great idea now, Caleb.'

'Why not?'

Folding her arms, she fixed him with a hard stare. 'Because of what's happened here, with us. To be honest, I'd be a little nervous about mixing a business partner-ship with a personal one. What if things went wrong between us? It's a risk.'

He shook his head. 'You can't worry about that. We're adults. We can keep the two things separate. I can't imagine any-thing that could tear us apart now.'

Moving closer to her, he put his finger under her chin and tipped it up so she had to look right into his eyes. 'I think I've got a pretty good measure of you, Elena Jones, and I want us to move forward—together. What happened in the past doesn't matter any more. I want you to believe that.'

'I do believe that,' she murmured, tears welling in her eyes.

'Then trust me. Trust us.'

After a small pause filled with almost painful expectancy, she smiled and said, 'Yes, okay. I trust us.'

He nodded, feeling his heart turn over with relief. 'I'll talk to the team tomorrow about working out a partnership agreement.' He held up a finger. 'On one condition.'

Blinking away the tears, she raised her eyebrows in anticipation.

'That you agree to stay here for the rest

of the week and go out with me tomorrow evening for Valentine's night. I've booked a table at Hora; it's the best Michelin-starred restaurant in town.'

Elena gazed at Caleb, her heart hammering hard in her chest, barely able to believe that her fortunes could have changed so significantly in the space of a few days. Blessed relief at the thought that she might now have a way to save her business and the livelihoods of her workforce cascaded through her.

Pulling him roughly to her, she dropped kisses all over his face until he started to laugh. 'I'd love to go to dinner with you. I've never been out on Valentine's Day before. Jimmy thought it was just a big marketing ploy to pressure men into spending ridiculous amounts of money on their girlfriends just to boost the big businesses' coffers.'

'Hmm, no wonder you left him—what a loser,' he said, running his fingers into her hair and looking deeply into her eyes. 'You deserve to be worshipped in every way possible, Elena Jones.'

The last of the worry she'd been carrying on her shoulders finally lifted, leaving her euphoric and light-headed.

Could this really be happening? Was it possible she'd not only found a way to save her business and quite likely propel it into a hugely successful venture with Araya Industries' help, but that she'd also got Caleb back into the bargain?

A small voice in her head told her not to get too excited about that last part just yet. It was still early days, and it had all moved so fast. While he seemed intent on rebuilding their fractured relationship right now, she was aware that he might change his mind once the first flush of excitement had worn off.

Although, perhaps the accident really had made him reconsider his whole outlook on life. Maybe he was tired of carrying around the anger and resentment that had broken their connection in the first place and was genuinely taking her advice about being more positive.

But she still couldn't help but worry that it could all change again in the blink of an eye.

She'd just have to be careful.

Though she knew deep down that she was probably far too late to rein back her feelings now.

She knew exactly what this feeling was that warmed her heart and lifted her soul.

She was in love with him.

And always had been.

When she zoned back in she realised he was looking at her with a mixture of concern and amusement.

'Are you okay? Have I blown your mind?' he asked with laughter in his voice.

A shiver of delight ran through her. It was so wonderful to see him happy again.

'Yes,' she said, returning his smile, 'but in the very best way.'

'Good.'

She took a breath and clapped her hands onto her knees. 'Well, if I'm going to stay here for a bit longer and go out for a fancy meal to celebrate with you tomorrow I'm going to need to buy more clothes. I only brought enough for a couple of days.'

'Okay. I can recommend a few places in the city to look for some,' he said, shifting closer to her. 'There are some great independent boutiques in the Gothic Quarter. But for now,' he murmured, reaching out a hand to trace the dips and hollows of her throat and shoulder blades with his fingertips, sending waves of pleasure rushing through her body, 'I think we should celebrate our partnership in a very different, but just as appropriate, way.'

'Sounds like a wonderful idea to me,' she said with a smile, then pressed her mouth hard to his, sinking into the heady reassurance of his embrace.

CHAPTER NINE

THE BOUTIQUE CLOTHES shops that Caleb had recommended were exactly what Elena was looking for and she spent a happy couple of hours browsing through rails of perfectly tailored dresses in a range of delicate, lush materials, heartened by the knowledge that he was so tuned in to her taste. There was something rather wonderful about being so well understood.

It had been a long time since she'd felt this excited about picking out new clothes for a date; in fact, it had been a long time since she'd even gone shopping like this, preferring to buy her clothes over the Internet for speed and efficiency.

Her friend Hannah had often tried to get her to join her at the weekends to browse through the stores and go for long, lazy lunches, but Elena had always been up to her eyeballs in work and had felt that going shopping would be a waste of her time.

How could she have allowed herself to become so practical? So insular. So narrow-minded? It was such a waste of her younger years, spending all her time focused on work instead of enjoying the friendships and opportunities for fun that she had at her fingertips. This time she'd spent with Caleb had really brought that to the fore for her and she challenged herself to make more of her time outside of work from now on.

Hopefully with Caleb there to enjoy it alongside her.

She didn't like to think about how they were going to make a long distance relationship work when they were both so busy with their businesses, but she guessed if they were both fully invested in it they'd make it happen somehow. In fact she rather liked the idea of moving to Barcelona to be near him. Once the Zipabout car had its battery and had been released onto the market she'd be looking for a new project to start on anyway. The rest of her team could handle the day-to-day running of the sales and marketing side so she could work on new ideas remotely, at least to begin with.

But she was getting ahead of herself here. Caleb hadn't talked about continuing their relationship past the end of this week and she'd be a fool to start planning her whole future around him.

Even if she wanted to. Very, very much.

She'd never felt more alive and excited about life than when she was with him. He had a way of bringing out the very best in her.

After choosing some new outfits and underwear to last her for the rest of the week she popped into a perfumery, which she'd spotted on one of the small side streets on her way there, sniffing at each of the bottles with delight and trying to identify the main ingredients in them.

Something shifted strangely inside her as she picked up a small, dark bottle in the shape of a swan. There was something incredibly familiar about it. Lifting it to her nose, she realised with a shock that she recognised the fragrance. It was one that Caleb had bought for her for a Christmas present, before they'd fallen out with each other. It had been the most exquisite thing she'd ever smelt and the revealing gesture of him taking the time to pick out and give her such a personal and intimate present had been the thing that had pushed her to finally admit how she really felt about him. She'd worn it on her skin for the whole week leading up to the last day of term, after they'd had their heart-to-heart about how they were perfect for each other and she'd promised him she'd finish her relationship with Jimmy as soon as she got home.

After she'd failed to come through on that promise and Caleb had made it clear he wanted nothing more to do with her she'd felt sick with shame and sadness every time she smelled that scent and had thrown it away.

She'd regretted that rashness for a long time afterwards though. In the end it was the only thing she'd had left to remind her of him. Despite repeated attempts to contact him and apologise, once he'd gone back to Spain she'd never heard from him again. It had been as if he'd never existed.

Smelling the scent again now brought back her intensely confused feelings of desperation to be with him, despite her fears that they just weren't practically suited. A memory of him drawing her close, leaning in on the pretext of smelling the perfume on her neck and instead brushing his lips against her skin, flashed across her mind. It had been one of the happiest, most intimate, most electrifying moments of her life.

She'd often wished she could have bottled that feeling to remind her of happier times.

And now she had it, right here in her hand.

Striding over to the counter, she handed the perfume to the sales assistant and drew her purse out of her bag.

'I've been searching for this for years,' she said, giving the woman a delighted grin. 'I'm so happy I've finally found it again.'

Caleb spent the day at work after calling his colleagues into a meeting to discuss how they'd move forward with both the partnership with the Americans and also with Elena's company.

He'd set the tone at the very beginning by being more friendly and relaxed than usual and had smiled to himself as he'd caught the looks of bemusement and surprise that had passed between his colleagues.

There had been a real buzz of excitement in the room as he laid out what had happened in the last few days. He'd made a point of taking a step back so that the project managers had a chance to take the lead, even though he itched to stay fully in control, and it had yielded great results. They were all smiling and buoyed up by the time the meeting concluded, which, he realised with a shock of sudden insight, was an unusual occurrence. Before he would have left the roomful of people a little subdued after he'd demanded their best from them. Today he'd let *them* decide to do the best job they could, and it seemed to have paid off.

He'd learnt an important lesson recently about taking a less aggressive attitude towards business and he knew he had Elena to thank for that.

She was good for him—helped balance him somehow.

He showered and changed at work, putting on his best casual suit for dinner, aware of a low level of excitement about seeing

Elena again this evening that had buzzed through his veins all day.

The traffic was bad and he tapped his fingers impatiently against the armrest of the car as his driver wound slowly through the early evening traffic.

'It looks like everyone's out for Valentine's night, clogging up the roads,' the driver muttered.

Caleb smiled at his grumpiness, thinking how great it was to be one of the people looking forward to an evening of romance for once.

Striding through the entrance of the restaurant, he bumped into a couple of people he knew socially who were also there for a romantic meal and they exchanged pleasantries, Caleb's pulse jumping with impatience to see Elena again after spending the day away from her.

He appeared to have turned into a teenager again. Not that he could remember those years clearly. Bits and pieces had come back to him over the last couple of days, mostly feelings of not having fitted in to a small, close-knit community in the small town where he'd been raised, a few miles west of Barcelona.

It was strange, but he was aware that this bothered him much less now—now he knew he'd made something of himself and proved all those naysayers wrong about him. Now that he had Elena.

Finally finding an out in the conversation so he could say a polite farewell to his acquaintances, he made his way towards the maître d's desk, where he was greeted with a smile of reverence and a warm welcome before being shown towards his table where, he was told, Elena was already waiting for him.

He'd chosen this restaurant because he liked its clean lines and no fuss décor, with its wall of glass which looked out onto a courtyard of flowers and olive trees, which were lit up tonight like some magical grotto. The simple wooden spoke-back chairs juxtaposed sharply with the pristine white tablecloths and blank walls, giving it all an understated but refined air. It was classy without being showy and he knew from experience that the food here was out of this world.

The perfect place to celebrate with Elena.

The table where she'd been seated was right next to the glass wall and the candle that flickered in front of her threw shadows onto the reflective surface, making it look as though she was sitting next to her ghostly double.

When she spotted him she stood up and smiled and his pulse skittered then began to jump in his throat. Gazing at her now brought home to him just how truly beautiful she was. Tonight she was wearing a fitted cocktail dress in a deep turquoise colour that made her iridescent eyes glow with warmth. Her pale golden hair flowed around her shoulders in waves, looking so lustrous in the soft light he ached to run his fingers through it.

In fact his overriding instinct right that second was to drag her into his arms and never let her go.

As he reached the table she stepped to the side and opened her arms for him to walk into her embrace, a wide smile playing about her lips and pleasure flashing in her eyes.

He dragged her roughly to him, burying his face in her hair and whispering, 'I missed you today.'

'I missed you too,' she murmured back.

He dragged in a deep breath, desperate to fill his senses with her soft, familiar scent—

And suddenly everything felt wrong.

His vision swam in front of him and a slow sinking sensation began to pull him down towards the floor.

That scent.

He knew it.

He *knew* it, but he didn't know why.

There was something completely wrong about it, but also completely right.

Elena and that scent went together.

But not in a good way.

Images began to cloud his mind's eye: of the two of them at university, studying in each other's rooms, laughing together. He felt flashes of happiness, then insecurity, then a cold hard rage that swelled up from somewhere deep inside him, dragging the breath from his lungs.

'Caleb? What's wrong?'

He heard Elena's voice as if it was coming to him from a distance. Nausea welled in his gut and he pushed her away from him, needing to be free of her hold, to get away from the smell that was causing his mind to rebel against him. His head pounded as if his brain had suddenly swollen and was pressing against the walls of his skull, the pain so intense he stumbled forwards, grabbing a chair to steady himself.

He felt her hand on his shoulder but he shrugged her off, not wanting her to touch him.

Then, like a floodgate opening, it all came rushing back: the soul-crushing disappointment and the hurt and humiliation he'd endured after he'd opened himself up to loving her back then. The way he'd trusted her implicitly with his heart and she'd taken it, played with it for a while then smashed it to pieces at his feet.

He'd made a total fool of himself for her.

After leading him to believe she cared about him as much as he did her and promising to come back after the Christmas holidays free to be with him, he'd gone home to Spain for the holidays, actually feeling happy for once to be going back there so he could tell his mother about the woman he'd fallen in love with.

She'd been so pleased for him; in fact it had been the first time they'd connected on any kind of emotional level since he'd been a young boy, perhaps because he finally understood how she could love someone so much she would do whatever it took to have them—that loving someone would be worth being estranged from others for.

After what had seemed like an interminable amount of time at home he'd gone back to Cambridge, desperate to see Elena after having promised not to call her whilst she was at home, to give her the time and space to deal with breaking up with Jimmy in a gentle and kind manner, only to find she was avoiding him.

He'd thought he was being paranoid at first, that it was bad timing when he kept missing her at her college. Until he'd finally tracked her down, panic surging through his veins, and she'd been visibly reluctant to see or speak to him. The cold distant look in her eyes had sent shivers of horror through him, which only increased when she'd told him in a toneless voice how she'd decided to stay with Jimmy after all, how she felt that he, Caleb, was too wild for her, too dangerous a proposition, too unpredictable. She needed to be with someone like Jimmy because she needed stability and calm in her life.

He'd felt belittled, rejected, foolish, but most of all heartsick at losing the woman he'd felt so sure felt the same way he did.

Taking a deep, much-needed breath, he finally straightened and turned to look into Elena's beautiful, deceitful face, feeling a deep, hot rage overtake him.

It hadn't been an undeniable romantic attraction that had connected them with such intensity over these last few days: it had been hatred.

'I remember, Elena,' he said, his voice raspy and strained as he forced the words past his throat. 'I remember why we stopped being *friends*.' He spat the last word out, feeling disgusted with himself for allowing her to take him in like this.

She'd used his memory loss against him to wheedle out what she wanted from him. And he, like a fool, had fallen for it. Fallen for her. Again.

'What are you talking about? Caleb, I don't understand. What just happened here?'

She looked panicked by his pronouncement, as well she should.

He crossed his arms. 'I know exactly what's been happening over the last few days. You've been using the fallout from the accident to get close to me.'

She stared at him, her cheeks flushed with colour and her brow pinched so tightly white lines formed on her skin.

'Did you invite me here tonight to humiliate me in public? To pay me back for what happened fifteen years ago?' she whispered, blinking as if trying to hold back tears.

He pushed away a sting of misplaced concern, forcing himself to remember that she was the one in the wrong here. 'No, of course not! I only remembered it all just now. The perfume you're wearing… It triggered something.' His head gave another throb of pain and he squeezed his eyes shut until it receded.

'Caleb? Are you okay?' The worry in her voice hit him straight in the chest, winding him.

'I'm fine,' he growled, not wanting to feel the way she was making him feel with her concerned, soothing *act*. The only person she'd ever cared about was herself and he needed to remember that.

'I see you for what you really are now, Elena,' he bit out angrily.

She swallowed hard, her face blanching, and glanced around her anxiously.

He suddenly realised that the room had become awfully quiet. When he looked round he saw that all the diners near them were staring their way in morbid fascination.

'Look, shall we sit down and talk about this rationally?' Elena said with a quaver in her voice, pulling out her chair with a shaking hand and sitting on it.

After a moment of indecision he pulled out his own chair and sat down opposite her, folding his arms. He was interested to hear how she was going to try and explain her self-serving actions away.

'What do you mean, you've only just remembered what happened?' she hissed, leaning forwards and putting her hands onto the table between them. 'You said your memory had fully come back!'

He shrugged dismissively. 'No. I lied about that. I didn't want you to think I was weak.' He leant back in his chair and narrowed his eyes at her. 'I pieced a story together from what you'd said about us and…' he paused, struggling to unclench his jaw to force out the name '…Jimmy. But I remember now. I remember the way you led me on then pushed me away when you changed your mind about who would serve your needs best.'

She held up both hands towards him in a halting gesture. 'I thought you understood how sorry I was about that. How I knew it had been the worst mistake of my life. I've been trying to make amends for the way I behaved then.'

'So you could manipulate me into getting what you wanted.'

Her hands bunched into fists now. 'No, Caleb, it wasn't like that.'

'So why did you stay after I'd told you I didn't want anything more to do with you and your business? Why were you so keen to look after me at the hospital?'

'Because I care about you, Caleb!' she shot back passionately. 'And there was a misunderstanding between the hospital staff about who I was to you that I got caught up in. But I was there because I felt awful about you getting hurt.'

'Because you were responsible for it.' It all made sense now. Cold, cruel sense.

'No! At least not directly. You were crossing the road to talk to me and you didn't look properly.'

'And why was that?'

She didn't seem to be able to meet his eye. 'I guess you were distracted.'

'You mean I was angry with you for not taking no for an answer?'

She visibly swallowed. 'Yes.'

'And then you stuck around when you thought I couldn't remember what had happened.'

'I was trying to make things right between us.'

'You mean when you realised I'd forgotten all about it you thought you'd be able to get what you wanted by pretending to care about me. By charming your way into my bed!'

Her eyes widened in dismay. 'What? No—!'

'I know exactly what you've been doing, Elena—you've been playing me this whole time, hoping to seduce me into giving you what you needed when I'd already told you no,' he bit out, anger and humiliation and heartache making his voice shake.

She gaped at him in stunned surprise, her face now bleached of colour. 'No, Caleb.' Her voice came out as a ragged whisper. 'That's not what happened!'

Elena felt sick.

How could he suddenly be acting so coldly towards her after the closeness they'd shared?

Who was she kidding? She knew how, because she'd done exactly the same thing to him fifteen years ago.

She swallowed hard, her mind whirring, trying to think of some way to convince him that she'd meant well by staying here to look after him and that she genuinely cared about him, but before she could say anything else he frowned, then shook his head as if another revelation had just struck him.

'You only went to that dinner meeting with Carter with me so I'd feel compelled to say yes to your own partnership.'

Gritting her teeth, she let out a moan of frustration. 'You asked me to go with you and I wanted to help you! Not for my own benefit, but for yours!'

He was nodding now though, as if he wasn't listening to her and things were suddenly making sense in his head. 'You guided me towards asking you to help me, planting the idea about me needing someone who understood the business. You manipulated me.'

'I did not,' she said as calmly as she could manage, trying like mad to control the shake of anger and hurt in her voice. 'It was your idea and there was no way I could refuse to help and leave you alone with your head injury. And I wanted to help, Caleb. Genuinely.'

He let out a low, disdainful laugh. 'Being genuine is not one of your strong points, Elena.'

'Maybe not fifteen years ago but, I promise you, it is now.'

'They why didn't you tell me everything when we had all our heart-to-hearts? There were plenty of opportunities.'

'Because I was afraid you'd kick me to the kerb. I was worried about you—about the fact you didn't seem to have anyone else to look after you. From what I've seen, you still seem intent on pushing away anyone who gets even vaguely close to you. I don't want you to end up old and alone. You deserve more than that. You deserve to be loved. And to be happy. You're a good man; you just need to believe it.'

He snorted. 'I know my own worth, Elena.'

'Do you?'

'Yes. *I* would never have slept with someone who couldn't remember the callous way I'd treated them in the past.'

She shoved her fingers into her hair in frustration. 'You told me you'd remembered.'

'Did you really believe I'd forgive you for the way you treated me back then, just like that?' He snapped his fingers, shooting her a look of disgust.

Dropping her head into her hands now, she let out a long, low sigh. 'I guess I knew deep down that something wasn't quite right, but I really wanted to believe things were okay with us again so I pushed any misgivings I had to one side.'

When she looked up again he was staring at her as if he didn't believe a word of it, his expression dark and unyielding.

'Yes, okay, I was being naïve,' she said, frustration making her belligerent now. 'It was wrong of me to let it happen.'

'So why did you?'

His question brought her up short. 'I—'

'You could have stopped me.'

'I couldn't. I didn't want to.'

'Why not, Elena?'

'Because I wanted you, all right!' she blurted, furious with herself for losing her cool.

'You wanted my battery, you mean,' he bit out, leaning towards her.

'No!' She took a breath, trying to calm her raging emotions. 'Well, yes. Okay.' She leant forwards too, fixing him with what she hoped was an honest and open expression. 'I need your battery because I have a lot of good people relying on me to find a way to save their jobs, but sleeping with you was a totally separate thing. I wanted to do it for me. For us.'

'For *us*?'

'Yes! I've missed you over the years and I didn't realise how much until I saw you again. How unhappy I was without you.'

There was a heavy beat of silence where

they stared at each other, their breathing rapid and the body language tense.

She thought she saw a flash of vulnerability in his eyes, but the next second it was gone, replaced with cool indifference. 'If you're saying that because you're worried I'm going to back out of the partnership then don't bother. I'm not that much of a monster,' he growled, reaching into his jacket and withdrawing a sheaf of papers, which he tossed onto the table in front of her. 'It's a contract I had drawn up earlier today which agrees to a partnership with your company.'

She stared at it in shock for a moment before dragging her gaze back to his.

'Caleb, thank you—'

But, before she could finish her sentence, he cut her off. 'My colleagues will be handling it from here so we won't need to have any more contact. I hope that makes you happy.'

She glared at him, her heart thumping against her chest and her jaw tight with frustration. 'Don't be ridiculous—of course it doesn't make me happy to not have any more contact with you!'

He huffed out a disdainful laugh, the expression in his eyes hauntingly distant, then without another word he went to stand up.

'Please, Caleb, stay,' she said desperately, reaching out a hand in an attempt to stall him. 'We need to talk more about this.'

'There's nothing left to say,' he stated coldly, brushing away her attempt to touch him and standing up, and before she could utter another word he turned and walked swiftly away from the table without looking back.

Elena sat there, numb with shock, battling down a painful ache deep inside her, afraid that once she let it rise to the surface she wouldn't be able to stop the tears that would inevitably come with it.

Everything might have just gone to hell but there was no way she was going to blub in the middle of a restaurant.

Gesturing to a passing waiter, she asked him to bring the bill for the champagne that she'd ordered and that neither of them had touched. She paid with her credit card, her movements jerky with anguish, then got up shakily and brushed herself down, setting back her shoulders before walking out of there, hyper-aware of the fascinated looks she was getting from the other diners.

Dumped on Valentine's night. It didn't get much more humiliating than that.

Once outside, she walked quickly down a side alley, away from prying eyes, and leant against the wall, burying her face in her hands.

But she refused to let herself cry.

She'd known, of course, on some subconscious level that Caleb had been lying about getting his memory back—that he'd been swept up in the excitement of closing the deal with the Americans and had wanted to celebrate with her the best way he knew how. And, to her shame, she'd let him, pretending to herself she believed that he remembered her even though he'd not remotely reacted in the way she'd been expecting.

Because she'd wanted him so badly she'd ached with longing.

The truth was, she'd been utterly selfish. She *had* taken advantage of his memory loss after the accident, not admitting it to herself at the time, but hoping—praying— it would never come back.

She'd brought all this on herself.

Just like she'd done fifteen years ago.

Caleb had trusted her implicitly then too, so much so he'd opened himself up to her—the first person he'd ever done that with after enduring such a punishing and isolated childhood—and she'd thrown his love and trust back in his face, deeming it worthless.

Then she'd hidden, like a coward, avoiding him at every turn until he'd been forced to come to her dorm room and practically break down the door to speak to her. She'd been afraid to face his disappointment in her so had put up a wall of ice to protect herself, telling him she'd made a mistake, he was too wild, too unpredictable for her, they could never be happy, not in the long run. She needed someone more stable, like Jimmy. He'd looked at her as if his world had just crashed in around him, before turning and walking away.

And that had been the last time he'd ever spoken to her. From that point on he'd acted as if she didn't exist. He'd looked through her as if she was nothing—a waste of space.

And she'd known deep down that she'd deserved it.

He'd practically gone to ground after that, skipping the lectures where she'd normally see him and never seeming to be at his dorm room when she dropped in, hoping to catch him and apologise and explain her horrible behaviour. And then he'd gone back to Spain as soon as the last lecture had finished, pushing past her when she'd tried to talk to him as if she meant nothing to him any more.

It had left an aching hole in her that had never closed over, even fifteen years later.

Because he'd been the love of her life.

It had tormented her more than she'd wanted to admit to herself over the years, chipping away at her self-respect, causing her to find fault in every man she'd dated, leaving her to wonder whether she'd ever be happy in a relationship again.

Until now.

But just when she'd thought she'd paid her dues and things were finally good between them again she'd lost him all over again.

CHAPTER TEN

CALEB MARCHED INTO his apartment, slamming the front door so hard behind him the angry sound of it reverberated around the space for a good few seconds.

How could he have let this happen? He'd known there was something strange going on but he'd blamed it on his memory loss instead of looking harder at the woman who had appeared out of nowhere like a ray of sunshine on a dark day.

Slumping onto the sofa, he winced in pain as his cracked rib reminded him that he'd been weakened by the accident in more ways than one.

But then hadn't he known, deep down, that there was more to her story than she was telling him and he'd let himself fall for her anyway?

Because he had—hard and intensely. The

thought of being with her had consumed him over the last few days, just like it had when he was younger. He knew why he'd not wanted to look too closely at what was going on. It was because he'd wanted her to be genuinely interested in exploring a relationship with him—wanted it more than he'd ever wanted anything in his life.

So he'd allowed himself to trust her, to begin to care about her—no, who was he kidding, he'd fallen in love with her and she'd used that to get what she wanted from him.

Once again she'd played him for a fool.

He felt as though his heart had been ripped from his chest. All that emotion that had been building inside him from the moment he'd seen her again swelled to an almost unbearable size, closing his throat, crushing his lungs, filling his head with unbearable pain.

No doubt she was already at the airport, ready to head home, happy in the knowledge that she'd achieved her objective here: to get him to sell her his battery, no matter what she'd had to do to get it.

Anger flashed through him, propelling

him off the sofa and towards his bedroom where her things were still hanging in his wardrobe and sitting on his shelves.

Well, he wanted them gone. He didn't want a trace of her left in his house now. He couldn't stand the pain of thinking about what he could have had if only she'd really wanted *him*.

Grabbing her small suitcase from where she'd stashed it in the wardrobe, he stuffed her clothes roughly into it willy-nilly, not caring how much it hurt his rib to do so—in fact, welcoming the pain it brought because it momentarily overrode the ache in his heart—then went to the bathroom and scooped all her toiletries into it too, forcing down the lid and roughly zipping it up.

Picking up the case, he strode to the front door, opened it, then tossed it into the hallway, where it bounced a couple of times before coming to rest on its side, looking battered and forlorn in the grandiose, brightly lit space.

Pushing away a rush of anguish, he slammed the door on it and strode into his kitchen, grabbing a glass tumbler out of the cupboard and splashing a good measure of whisky into it.

He knocked it back, feeling the burn in the back of his throat and registering the warmth as it hit his stomach, though deriving no pleasure from it whatsoever.

Pouring himself another large shot, he took it into the living area and slumped down onto the sofa again, staring out of the window at the dark night sky, which had become stormy with wind and rain that lashed against the glass, trying not to think about how painfully alone he was here in this big echoing apartment.

Despite the way Elena had treated him, his traitorous body still ached for her. His throat was tense from holding back the urge to rage and swear at the world, his chest tight with sorrow and frustration.

He knew, with ringing clarity now, why he'd deliberately sabotaged his engagement to his ex, Adela. He'd been afraid to trust her love for him for this very reason. His survival instinct had kicked in and he'd pushed her away before she could do it to him first.

Because he'd been afraid of something like this happening to him again.

The sad truth was he'd fallen for Adela in the first place because she'd reminded him of Elena. Adela had exhibited many of Elena's traits; she'd even looked a bit like her, but of course he knew deep down that she could never be her. That was why he'd broken off their engagement. It wouldn't have been fair to Adela to have always been second best in his heart.

Perhaps he was destined to always be alone. It would at least be easier that way. Like it had been when he was younger.

He was also acutely aware now that keeping his relationship with his mother at arm's length had had a serious effect on the way he dealt with all his close relationships to this day.

At least after her cancer was diagnosed he'd made sure to visit her more and they'd brokered a kind of unspoken peace between them. He'd never totally understood the life choices she'd made, but he'd come to finally accept them, and her. During those sad, desolate hours at the end of her life she'd made it clear to him that she'd always loved him and that she regretted the distance that had always been between them.

It had torn him up inside, the futility of it, because she was gone now and all he was left with was a sense of deep sorrow for the time he'd wasted spurning her instead of loving and accepting her for who she was.

And now he'd lost the woman he'd hoped to spend his future with too.

The woman he loved.

Knocking back the second whisky, he closed his eyes and tried to blank his mind of her—to shut out the pain and grief that made him feel as though someone had stripped him to the bone—but it was no good; he knew there was no forgetting Elena Jones.

Elena paced the streets, barely noticing the rain as it began to fall steadily from the sky, seeping into her new dress and plastering her hair to her head.

How could things have gone so wrong so quickly? She'd known before, of course, that there was a chance they might when she'd thought his memory was still missing, but for him to have lied about remembering her, then shown her how wonderful they could be together, only then to regain his memory and reject her was devastating.

Lightning flashed overhead, shocking her out of her frustrated, meandering thoughts, and she ducked under a nearby awning of a restaurant where a few other tourists had gathered, taking shelter from the storm. What was she doing? Moping around Barcelona in the rain wasn't going to solve the problem; the only way she was going to get him to listen to her was to turn up at his apartment and refuse to leave until he did.

She wasn't going to run from him again, not this time. She was going to do what she should have done all those years ago—be brave and fight for what she really wanted, no matter the consequences. She'd never be able to forgive herself if she didn't, not now she knew what she'd be missing—a positive, life-affirming partnership with the man she loved.

Seeing an available taxi driving down the street, she ran back out into the rain and hailed it, jumping into the back seat and giving the driver Caleb's address in a voice shaking with nerves and determination.

She would not give up on them. Not this time.

The journey seemed to take an age as they joined the slow-moving traffic and more and more people jumped into taxis to shelter from the rain. Elena tapped her foot anxiously, wondering what sort of reception she'd get when he opened the door and found her standing there. Would he be angry, cold, indifferent? Or, now that he'd had some time to calm down and reflect rationally on it all, would he be relieved to see her?

She hoped so.

Oh, how she hoped.

The taxi finally drew up outside his building and she shoved the fare towards the driver, telling him to keep the change in her haste to get to Caleb, and dashed across the pavement and up to the entry door to his block. Pulling out the spare key card that Caleb had lent her that morning, so she could get in and out while he was out at work, she pressed it against the pad and sighed with relief when the door lock clicked open. She wouldn't have put it past him to have the code reconfigured to keep her out.

The lift was already at ground level and it took her straight up to his apartment. Walking into the hallway, she came to a surprised stop when she saw a suitcase lying haphazardly in the middle of the floor. She frowned at the incongruity of it, wondering absent-mindedly what it was doing there. And then it hit her like a fist to the gut.

It was hers.

Caleb must have packed her things and thrown them out here in case she had the gall to return for them. Well, she wasn't going to let that deter her. Marching up to his door, she hammered loudly on it, her heart thumping in her throat as she stood there listening for his heavy footsteps coming towards her. It occurred to her wildly that she wasn't exactly looking her best at the moment—a lot like a drowned rat, in fact—but she shoved the thought away, knowing this was no time for vanity.

The door swung open and she looked up into Caleb's handsome face, forcing herself not to take a step backwards as she registered the anger in his expression.

'Your things are behind you in the hall,' he said curtly, the bitterness in his voice making her stomach roll.

'I'm not here for my things; I'm here for you,' she stated baldly, keeping her gaze locked with his and her chin determinedly up.

A range of expressions passed over his face: from bemusement to resentment and finally, and most worryingly, to incredulity.

'Let me in, Caleb,' she said calmly, but with a determination that rose from her very soul.

'You can say what you need to right here,' he said, folding his arms in front of him, effectively blocking her way past him with his enormous bulk.

The coldness in his eyes shook her, but there was no way she was going to let him scare her off now. She knew that the kind, compassionate man she'd got to know again over the last few days was still in there somewhere; she just needed to get him to hear what she had to say then maybe she'd be able to draw him back out again.

'Okay, fine, if it has to be said here in your hallway then it will be.' She took a breath and set back her shoulders.

'You were right; I wasn't honest with you and I should have been from the very start, but I was afraid you'd push me away and I desperately wanted to make up for the way I treated you in the past. I was selfish and cruel then but, please believe me, I'm not that same self-absorbed girl I used to be. I'm a different person now. A better one, I hope. Surely you've seen proof of that over the last few days.'

He didn't give any indication that she was getting through to him, his posture remaining stiff and his expression impassive, so she decided just to get it all out in the hope that something she said would strike a chord with him.

'I know I told you that I decided I couldn't marry Jimmy because our relationship was staid and—boring.' She winced at how awful that sounded. What a terrible person she'd been, to them both.

Caleb still didn't say anything, his expression remaining indifferent.

She took another steadying breath, then

let the words rush out. 'But the truth is, I broke up with him because I realised I'd never feel about him the way I felt about you.'

There was a flicker of something in his eyes and she held her breath for a moment, praying for a reaction, but he steadfastly refused to give her one.

Swallowing hard, she bunched her fists for courage.

'Back then I was afraid of how unpredictable you were, how you didn't fit into the way I'd envisioned my life turning out, but mostly how I still wanted you—desperately—despite all of that. After years of keeping a tight control over my life, that completely rattled me. So I stuck with Jimmy, the safe bet, the man I could control. Because I was a coward.'

He wasn't looking at her now, but staring off into the distance. Folding her arms, she steeled herself to hold it together.

'I realised later on, of course, once I'd grown up a little, that a certain amount of conflict can be good for a relationship. I guess it gives it the edge it needs to keep things exciting and fresh. As long as there's enough love between a couple…I think I mistook passion for dysfunction in my parents' marriage but they're still together today, so it shows what I know.'

She was aware that she was dripping water onto the floor now and that she'd begun to shiver with cold, but she pushed aside her discomfort, feeling it was probably a fitting state for her confession.

'I think I've really been single for so long because I stopped trusting my judgement when it comes to relationships. I was ashamed of the way I'd acted in the past and avoided getting close to anyone again in case I made the same mistakes. But after spending this incredible time with you here I realised that if I want to be happy it's time to stop being afraid of what might go wrong.'

She took a step closer to him. 'And embrace what could go right. Because I'm so happy when I'm with you.' Her voice broke as she took another step forwards and saw him tense, then tighten and raise his arms like a barrier.

'You really think I'm going to be able to trust you again?' he muttered.

'I do. Because I think you want to; it's just your pride getting in the way.'

'My *pride*? You broke your word to me and you lied; why should I believe you won't do that again?'

'Because I'm not the girl you remember, Caleb. I'm older and wiser now.' She took a deep, shaky breath. 'I was so ridiculously naïve back then, I had no idea what I really needed.' She gave him a beseeching smile, holding her breath as she waited to see whether she'd finally got through to him.

'You have to understand that you scared me at the time. You were so full of anger and bitterness I didn't know whether I could handle you. I wasn't a very strong person then.'

'I didn't need your strength, Elena. I needed your loyalty and respect.'

It felt as though his words had slapped her in the face. She knew he was right; she'd disrespected him in the worst possible way. He trusted her with the whole of his already damaged heart and she'd toyed with it for a while, then thrown it back at him, broken and beyond repair. It had been the worst thing she could have done to him; no wonder he'd turned into the hardened character she'd first met here last week.

'I don't blame you for being reluctant to trust my word after I made such a mess of things last time, but please, Caleb, *please* give me another chance.'

Her heart started to race and her body flushed hot with trepidation as she looked up into his hooded eyes and said, 'I love you.'

He stared at her, a deep frown marring his face.

'You *love* me?' His tone was so troubled her heart went right out to him.

'Yes, and I want us to make this relationship work.'

He shook his head, the expression in his eyes a little wild as if he was fighting with himself about how to respond.

Her chest gave a little jolt of hope at the thought that perhaps she might finally be getting through to him.

Turning away from her, he began to pace up and down the hall, raking his hands through his hair and making it stand on end. He looked troubled, anxious—but *encouraged* maybe?

'I don't know, Elena. It's a lot to process. I thought I knew you—'

'You *do* know me. Everything I've told you about myself is true. Everything we've done together has been genuine and came from a place of love and respect for you.'

Still he shook his head, as if not daring to believe it.

'I understand why you're feeling this way. It has to be so confusing losing your memory like that,' she said in desperation. 'Then finding out you were missing a big chunk of important information.' She walked to him now and put her hands on his arms, gripping them hard and using the whole of her strength to stop him from pacing.

'Listen to me, Caleb Araya. I am not letting you push me away again. I know I was in the wrong fifteen years ago, but everything that's happened between us in the last week has been real. And I think you feel the same, though you're too stubborn to admit it.'

Caleb stared at this brave, fierce woman in front of him and felt the heavy weight of unhappiness lift a little from his chest.

He knew what she was saying made sense; she'd been nothing but kind and caring towards him since leaving the hospital and he was acutely aware that he was letting his fear and panic get in the way of common sense. His chest gave a sharp throb as he accepted that if it hadn't been for her courage to stand up to him and assert her steadying influence at the meeting he would have lost Carter's business. She'd done that to help him. Because she cared about him. He knew that really, deep in his heart.

In reality, it had been his fault this had all turned into such an awful mess in the blink of an eye because he'd lied about his memory coming back so they could take their relationship further; and it had definitely been him who had asked her to go with him to the meeting with Carter. He remembered the look of wary uncertainty on her face now when he'd suggested it. That, he knew without a doubt, had been absolutely genuine.

He could recognise all that now—now he'd started to see through the fog of fear and panic that had engulfed him earlier.

Looking inside himself, he knew he'd

forgiven her a long time ago for what had happened between them. Really, he'd hated himself for being so weak and proud, but until now he'd been too afraid to admit it to himself because it was easier to hate someone than to admit how much you loved them. How much it tore you apart to not have that love returned.

A small defiant part of him still wanted to hang on to the animosity he'd hidden his feelings behind, to keep himself safe from any more pain and uncertainty, but he knew he couldn't do that. Not after she'd been brave enough to turn up here, dripping wet and bedraggled, to lay her heart at his feet when she could have just got on a plane with her signed contract and never had to face him again.

He wouldn't do that to her because what he wanted most in the world was a real and honest relationship with her, even if their journey together was likely to be littered with obstacles and challenges.

She made him happy.

He loved her and she loved him and when it came down to it that was all that really mattered.

Seeming to sense a softening in his attitude, she moved closer to him and tentatively raised a hand to his face. The warmth of her touch heated his skin, starting a fire in his chest which radiated out through his body until every centimetre of him ached to hold her against him again.

'Please, Caleb, please forgive me. Let me back in,' she whispered.

The crack of pain and desperation in her voice broke through the very last of his reserve and he felt the final tendrils of his anger leave him, washed away by the dizzying elation of her presence here—the place where she belonged.

Cupping her jaw in his hands, he smiled at her, drawing her closer. 'There's nothing to forgive. I've been wrong to hold what happened between us all those years ago against you, but it was easier to hate you than face what I'd become: a bitter, cold-hearted fool.'

She opened her mouth as if to disagree but he held up his hand, asking her to wait until he'd finished.

'Being with you has brought me alive again. I love being around you; the world feels like a better place when you're here.'

He frowned as he remembered the horrified look on her face in the restaurant just before he'd stormed away in angry confusion. 'When my memory came back earlier this evening I think I panicked. I suddenly had all these conflicting thoughts and feelings racing through my head, and I didn't know what was truth and what was fiction any more. My natural instinct was to push you away to protect myself. I was afraid you didn't really care about me the way I'd hoped you did and it scared the hell out of me.'

He stroked his thumbs across her cheeks, brushing away the tears that had begun to streak down her face.

'Because I love you, Elena,' he murmured, holding her gaze with his for one precious moment, seeing relief and love light up in her eyes, before bringing his mouth down to hers with a kiss that took his breath away at the utter perfection of it.

He felt her finally relax against him and he pulled her closer, wrapping his arms around her and pressing their bodies tightly together, feeling the strongest compulsion to never let her go again.

'Caleb, your rib,' she muttered against his shoulder where her face was squashed by his encircled arms.

'It's fine. Don't worry.'

'I don't want to hurt you,' she said, pulling away to look up into his face.

'You won't,' he said with conviction.

'You know, we're probably going to be one of those couples that constantly strikes sparks off each other,' she said with a hint of worry in her eyes.

'I hope so,' he said, dipping down to nuzzle her neck and feeling great satisfaction in the little shiver of enjoyment she gave. 'It will keep life exciting.'

'So we'll have to make sure our kids know how much we love each other,' she said with determination in her voice.

He drew back and raised both eyebrows. 'Kids?'

She nodded firmly. 'Yes. I want three.'

'That's brave,' he said, adding a wry lilt of humour to his voice, though deep down he knew that having children with her would make him the happiest man in the world. She'd be an incredible mother: caring, brave and compassionate, and would fight tooth and nail for her children's happiness and security, making sure they knew how loved they were, how wanted.

'I am brave now,' she said. 'I refuse to be afraid of the future any more. We'll take life as it comes, you and I, and deal with anything it throws at us together.'

'I like your style, Elena Jones,' he murmured, bending to kiss her hard and let her know just how much he meant that.

'And I like yours, Caleb Araya,' she said once she'd got her breath back.

And with that sentiment lifting his heart he took her hand in his and led her out of the cold empty hallway and into the shelter of his home.

EPILOGUE

Two years later

IT WAS UNSEASONABLY warm for London in February as Caleb strode through Green Park on his way to meet Elena by the Tube station and he loosened his tie and undid the top button of his shirt, finding relief as the gentle breeze hit his heated skin. He was taking her out for high tea at The Ritz to celebrate her recent design award for her Zipabout cars and was running a little late after a meeting in the City had gone on longer than he'd anticipated.

They'd both been astonished and delighted by the huge impact that the Zipabout cars had had on the electric car industry and Elena was already deep into the design and pre-manufacture of a new model on the back of its success. He was ridiculously proud of all she'd achieved and infinitely delighted to be able to say he'd played some small part in it.

He saw the cars everywhere he went now, both here in England, where they spent big chunks of time in order for Elena to keep in close contact with her company, and also in Spain, where they'd made a permanent home together in the Pedralbes area in the district of Les Corts, which they'd chosen for its wide avenues and green open spaces as well as the spectacular views towards Barcelona.

He hadn't needed much persuasion to move from his rather sequestered, cavernous flat in L'Eixample and into a comfortable four-bed house set within a friendly community of families and professionals, and for the first time in his life he felt truly settled where he lived. Content.

As he rounded the bend near the station his gaze alighted on a figure walking towards him, her long blonde hair glowing in the soft winter sunshine and her cheeks flushed with colour.

The most beautiful woman in the world. His wife.

She waved when she saw him, her mouth curving into a beatific smile that both melted his heart and made his pulse race. Despite all the time they spent together now, he still hated being separated from her, rushing at the end of each day to get back home. Not a day went by when he didn't thank his lucky stars for the accident that had brought them together, even if it had been in the most dramatic and extraordinary of ways.

Blessedly, he'd been physically fine after all the bruising had finally gone down and after a few more weeks the rest of his memory had returned in full, along with a sense of regret for all the time he'd spent hanging on to the anger from his past that had kept him so isolated from the rest of the world.

But there were no regrets about his life now.

There were times, of course, when he and Elena butted heads but, instead of being afraid of the conflict they embraced it, getting any bottled-up feelings out into the open and using it as a kind of catharsis. They found as long as they kept communicating they were able to work through anything that crossed their path and Caleb made sure to tell Elena every day just how much he loved her.

Returning her smile, he glanced down in love-struck awe at her belly, which was straining against the trench coat she was wearing. In about three months' time there would be someone else for him to love with the same kind of fierce abandon too. Their child.

'Hello, beautiful,' he said as they reached each other and he drew her towards him for a kiss, savouring the feel of her mouth on his and breathing in her reassuring scent.

'How was your meeting?' she asked with a breathy laugh when he finally let her go.

'It went well, I think, though they were more impressed by the fact I'm married to you,' he said, gently brushing her hair away from her face to gaze into her eyes. 'My incredible, talented wife.'

She raised both eyebrows in an expression of wry modesty, then smiled, unable to keep a straight face. 'I couldn't have done it without you,' she murmured, sliding her hands up to cup his jaw and leaning forwards to kiss him firmly on the lips. 'So let's go and celebrate our perfect partnership.'

And with that they linked hands and walked together to their next destination, driven on by the excitement of all the new adventures they had lying ahead of them.

* * * * *

If you enjoyed this book by
Christy McKellen, look out for
A COUNTESS FOR CHRISTMAS
also by Christy McKellen

Or if you enjoyed this
gorgeous Mediterranean hero,
look out for another in
HER FIRST-DATE HONEYMOON
by Katrina Cudmore

Both available as ebooks!

COMING NEXT MONTH FROM

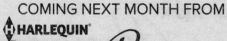

Available November 8, 2016

#4543 CHRISTMAS BABY FOR THE PRINCESS
Royal House of Corinthia • by Barbara Wallace

Pregnant Princess Arianna flees to New York, set against marrying the man who deceived her. But when she finds herself penniless, handsome restaurateur Max Brown can't resist rescuing her! But is his mysterious new waitress here for life—or just for Christmas?

#4544 GREEK TYCOON'S MISTLETOE PROPOSAL
Maids Under the Mistletoe • by Kandy Shepherd

When guarded billionaire Lukas Christophedes finds maid Ashleigh Murphy living in his mansion, he strikes a deal—she can stay if she acts as his girlfriend. But lines quickly start to blur, and Ashleigh starts wishing for a more heartfelt proposal...

#4545 THE BILLIONAIRE'S PRIZE
by Rebecca Winters

Dea Caracciolo has spent her whole life feeling inferior—and never more so than when she first met billionaire Guido Rossano. For Guido, enchanting Dea is the one who got away. When fate throws them together, Guido decides to take his prize—
Dea as his wife!

#4546 THE EARL'S SNOW-KISSED PROPOSAL
by Nina Milne

Gabriel, Earl of Wycliffe, hires historian Etta Mason to research his family tree and find him an heir! They might be spending Christmas in Vienna, but single mom Etta doesn't believe in fairy-tale endings. Even still, she can't help but be tempted by his achingly romantic kisses...

HRLPCNM1016

HARLEQUIN® Romance

Next month, Harlequin® Romance author

Jennifer Faye

brings you the first book in her Mirraccino Marriages duet:

The Millionaire's Royal Rescue

Tempted by the rebellious royal…

Billionaire Grayson Landers has fled the paparazzi back home—only to find himself in another media storm: rescuing the king's niece from a thief!

Lady Annabelle DiSalvo is no pampered princess—she's come to the Mediterranean island of Mirraccino to solve the mystery of her mother's death. Grayson can't help but want to help her. Plagued by guilt over not being able to save his ex, this is his chance for redemption. Only he absolutely cannot fall for her and risk his heart again…*unless it's already too late!*

**On sale March 2017,
only from Harlequin® Romance.
Don't miss it!**

Mirraccino Marriages
Royal weddings in the Mediterranean

**And look out for the second book in the
Mirraccino Marriages duet by Jennifer Faye.
On sale June 2017.**

*Available wherever Harlequin® Romance books
and ebooks are sold.*

*Pastry chef Gemma Rizzo never expected to see
Vincenzo Gagliardi again. And now he's not just the
duke who left her brokenhearted...he's her new boss!*

RETURN OF HER ITALIAN DUKE,
the first book in **The Billionaire's Club** trilogy
by *Rebecca Winters*.

Read on for a sneak preview:

Since he'd returned to Italy, thoughts of Gemma had
come back full force. At times he'd been so preoccupied,
the guys were probably ready to give up on him. To think
that after all this time and searching for her, she was right
here. Bracing himself, he took the few steps necessary to
reach Takis's office.

With the door ajar he could see a polished-looking
woman in a blue-and-white suit with dark honey-blond
hair falling to her shoulders. She stood near the desk with
her head bowed, so he couldn't yet see her profile.

Vincenzo swallowed hard to realize Gemma was no
longer the teenager with short hair he used to spot when
she came bounding up the stone steps of the *castello*
from school wearing her uniform. She'd grown into a
curvaceous woman.

"Gemma." He said her name, but it came out gravelly.

A sharp intake of breath reverberated in the office. She
wheeled around. Those unforgettable brilliant green eyes

with the darker green rims fastened on him. A stillness seemed to surround her. She grabbed hold of the desk.

"Vincenzo... I—I think I must be hallucinating."

"I'm in the same condition." His gaze fell on the lips he'd kissed that unforgettable night. Their shape hadn't changed, nor the lovely mold of her facial features.

She appeared to have trouble catching her breath. "What's going on? I don't understand."

"Please sit down and I'll tell you."

He could see she was trembling. When she didn't do his bidding, he said, "I have a better idea. Let's go for a ride in my car. It's parked out front. We'll drive to the lake at the back of the estate, where no one will bother us. Maybe by the time we reach it, your shock will have worn off enough to talk to me."

Hectic color spilled into her cheeks. "Surely you're joking. After ten years of silence, you suddenly show up here this morning, honestly thinking I would go anywhere with you?"

Make sure to read...
RETURN OF HER ITALIAN DUKE by Rebecca Winters,
available March 2017 wherever
Harlequin® Romance books and ebooks are sold.

www.Harlequin.com